MURDER UNDER THE WINDOW

By

Wanda Raboteau Heath

MURDER UNDER THE WINDOW

Wanda Raboteau Heath

Lepaugene' Enterprises, LLC
P.O. Box 640842
Kenner, LA 70064
Lepaugene@aol.com

MURDER UNDER THE WINDOW

Copyright©2002
By
Wanda Raboteau Heath

This novel is a work of fiction

Names, characters, places and incidents either are products of the author's
imagination or are used fictitiously. Any resemblance to actual persons,
living or dead, events or locales is entirely coincidental.

Library of Congress Control Number: 2002 141233

ISBN: 0-9720106-0-2

Cover Design: Charles E. Joseph, Brazen Images

Printed in the United States of America
by
Morris Publishing
3212 E Highway 30
Kearney, NE 68847
800-650-7888

DEDICATION

To my grandchildren, with deepest love.

Deven
Brandena
Kendall
Paul, Jr.
Isabella

* * * *

In memory of my parents.

Genevieve and Leo Paul Raboteau

ABOUT THE AUTHOR

Wanda Raboteau Heath, a native of Bay St. Louis, Ms currently resides in Kenner, La. She is the founder and owner of Lepaugene' Enterprises, LLC.

For the past thirty-seven years, Wanda has worked in hospitals as Director of Health Information Management Departments (formerly, Medical Record Departments). During this time she has served on local, state and national committees for Health Information Management Associations.. She recently served as National President of the Esther Mayo Sherard Foundation that awards scholarships to students pursuing degrees in Health Information Management. Wanda is very proud to be a charter member of this organization and honored to have served as President when the first scholarship was awarded.

In October, 2001, Wanda retired from Ochsner Hospital, New Orleans, Louisiana after serving twenty-two years as Director of Health Information Management. To launch her second career, she has written her first novel, *Murder Under The Window*. Prior to the release of this book, Wanda has written two personalized books, *Loving Hands* and *Kendall 's Birthday Celebration* for the children in her extended family.

She has two sons, two daughters-in-law and five grandchildren.

THE

AUTHOR

THANKS.......

....God for allowing His hand to be with me.

....Frank, Jr. and Paul, who are my sons, my supporters, my teachers, my friends, my comforters, my protectors and my role models who encouraged me "to do my own thing, to work for myself, to enjoy my retirement and just be happy."

.... Tracy and Charles Joseph, who are my editors, my photographers, my friends, and my niece and nephew-in-law who gave their insight, guidance, encouragement and support through every step of the publishing process.

....Contessa Wall, who is my instructor and my mentor who became my friend who unselfishly shared her knowledge of Self-Publishing with me and taught me how to make my dream become a reality.

....Marilyn Bateman, my former co-worker and now my final editor who unselfishly gave up her time to carefully review and edit *Murder Under The Window*.

....Jeanette Pitt, my friend of thirty-five years, who was the first to struggle to read my handwritten manuscript scribbled in two composition books and the first to recommend to me to "get this book published."

....Toya LaBostrie, my little cousin who deciphered my handwriting and entered the first draft of my book into the computer.

....Mary Clarke, my Aunt, and my first editor who encouraged me not only on this project, but also through my adult life.

....You, my reader for buying my book and sharing your valuable time with me as you peer through the shadowy windows down my path of make believe.

I love you and I thank you!

Wanda Raboteau Heath

FOREWORD

by Contesse' Wall

Murder Under The Window is overflowing with passion, intrigue, courage and wisdom. The anticipation of turning every page explodes with exuberance and a curiosity that grabs the reader by the edge of his seat. The twists and turns throughout *Murder Under The Window* are reflective of creativity at its best!

The enduring love and strength of the family unit portrayed in this dynamic story and their ability to support and encourage each other through a devastating ordeal catapults their sense of togetherness into new heights. The coming together to draw upon each other when things go awry is exemplified with terrific love and compassion.

Murder Under The Window taps deep into the soul and triggers a thirst for more and more. This unique book teaches lesson after lesson in the human feelings we experience when something tragic happens and we begin to unravel.

We search for answers and rationale but oftentimes we don't find what we're looking for. Therefore, we have to settle for what exists and accept that there are things that will happen in life we can't change. We do however, find ways to cope with these changes through faith and hope.

Murder Under The Window demonstrates a celebration of life and family. The perseverance of a family's ability to rise above obstacles, pain and fear is inspirational and heartwarming. The tears of joy and pain from the tragic unfolding of events in the plot remind each of us that the precious vulnerability of human life is very fragile.

The emotional roller coaster in Murder Under The Window cautiously wraps around the fragile emotions of life through mystery, addiction, social injustice and the heartache of loss. The trials and tribulations in this heart wrenching story grabs your imagination with an overzealous manipulation and takes you on a very mysterious journey, while illustrating the precious gift of life.

MURDER UNDER THE WINDOW

CHAPTER
ONE

"Baby, please, you have to help yourself. Talk to me. I know that you didn't commit this heinous crime but I need you to help prove it. You know I love you and our entire family loves you. Darling, I need you now more than ever since your mother is no longer with us."

"Please, Daddy, go away. I need to be alone." Joseph Morgan stared at his daughter, Janita, in disbelief and his eyes began to swell with tears. Janita turned and slowly walked to the prison guard without looking back at her father. She could not stand to see the man she loved so dearly hurt so much. Joseph watched his daughter as she walked away, until he could no longer see her. Trying to hold back tears he slowly walked through the prison doors to his car.

Alone in the car, Joseph sobbed and wondered what had happened to his family and what he could do to help bring peace in a time of so much turmoil. His mind drifted back to his beautiful daughter that he had just left behind bars. He made a promise to Jacquelyn, his deceased wife, that he would get Janita out of jail and also prove her innocence.

Joseph picked up his cellular phone and dialed a number. Immediately he heard the voice of Joseph Junior, his first-born.

"What's up, Pop?"

"Junior, are you psychic or what? How did you know that I was calling?"

"Pop, get with it. I told you to stop being cheap and spend a few dollars more each month to get caller ID."

"Boy, that is foolish, I'll know who's calling as soon as the caller says hello. Remember, son, a few dollars saved each month will add up to be more than a few dollars in a year and

1

after several years, those few dollars saved could be a lot of money."

"Yeah, yeah, Pop, why don't you admit it, you are just cheap. Pop, where are you?"

"I just visited with your sister and I am now leaving the jail. Son, can you get the family together so that we can meet as soon as possible? Janita needs the family and we really need to discuss what has happened."

"Sure, Pop." I'm sure I can locate the others and we can probably be there in two hours. The sooner, the better, right, Pop?"

"Right, Son. I'll see you in two hours. Good-bye."

Joseph smiled and thought how blessed he and his late wife had been with their four children and he whispered, "Thank you Lord for allowing me to raise your children for you. They are all so special and are so giving in a time of crisis." Joseph made another call to his secretary, Melrose Clark, and asked that she contact Attorney Jeff Spratt to make an urgent appointment with him for today, early afternoon.

Joseph looked at his watch and realized that he would have enough time to attend morning Mass at his neighborhood church. Following Mass, Joseph went directly home to prepare for the family meeting. He checked his telephone messages and his first call was from his secretary confirming a one o'clock luncheon meeting with Attorney Spratt. The meeting would be in Spratt's office and lunch would be delivered to them there.

At exactly ten thirty, Joseph Jr., Julie and Jeanette walked into the den of their father's home. As Joseph ushered his children into his office, he thanked each one for agreeing to come to the meeting on such a short notice.

Joseph had set up his office as a meeting room with tape recorder, flip charts and three chairs arranged in a semi-circle. Junior moved his sister, Julie to the middle chair and he and Jeanette sat on each side of their sister.

"Julie, how are you doing?" Joseph asked.

"Pop, I'm okay."

2

Joseph announced that this meeting would have to be over by noon because he had a luncheon meeting scheduled with Jeff Spratt.

"Daddy", Jeanette cried, "please, do something. I miss my sister and it hurts so much just thinking about her in that awful place."

Julie added, "This has to be solved soon because it is affecting my marriage. Malcolm cannot understand how I can try to help Janita when he and I are still in mourning."

With a feeling of helplessness, Joseph looked at his distraught daughter and whispered, "Baby, I am so sorry but I promise you that we are going to fix this situation soon."

Junior said, "Julie, please interrupt this meeting at any time that the discussions get too difficult for you to handle. We will all understand."

Julie whispered, "Pop, let's get started."

CHAPTER
TWO

Attorney Spratt walked into his secretary, Amy Rollins's office and said, "We need to be prepared for my meeting with Joe Morgan. Please contact Paul Mason, the private investigator that we used on the Williams case and ask him if he could meet with me this afternoon, in my office. Also, please find out the status of Janita Morgan's case. Call our contacts at the north-side police station and gather as much information as you can about this case. I need as much information as I can get about the evidence before the meeting. Did you order lunch?"

"No. Joe's secretary, Melrose, wanted to do it because she was familiar with all of your favorite foods."

Jeff, smiled as he thought, "Melrose is as organized as her boss." He said to Amy, "Please give Paul Mason the name of the case. I am sure that he will want to be prepared when he meets with me. By the way, have you added any other appointments to my schedule for today?"

"Actually, it's open because you had planned on visiting and touring the fitness center to decide if you wanted to join it."

"Good, cancel that because I'd like to go down to Court Street to see if they will allow me to see Janita Morgan. Technically, I'm not her attorney, yet but some of the men over there owe me a few favors and I think I'll cash them in on this case."

"Do you think she will see you?"

"I'm sure that I can convince her to see her favorite Uncle Jeff. Amy, I should be back in about an hour but if you need me, you can reach me on my cell phone."

4

As Spratt parked his new Mercedes in front of the police station, several patrolmen made comments about the beautiful champagne convertible car. Teasingly, Jeff tossed the keys to one of the guys he recognized.

"Try it out but have it back by the time I return."

They all laughed and tossed the keys back to Jeff. Jeff thought, "I might need them in the very near future so I had better make sure they are comfortable with me." Jeff opened the front door of the precinct station and Ronnie Petit, the Chief of Police, walked up to him and the two men shook hands.

"What can I do for you today, my friend?"

"Hi, Ronnie, I'm here to see Janita Morgan."

"Are you representing her?"

"Not yet, but I'm meeting with Joe this afternoon and if I'm asked you know that I will agree to be her lawyer."

"Just make sure that you're not too close to the case."

"Thanks for the advice."

"Come on, I'll walk with you to meet her. Jeff, this case will be very difficult for you and me and I think that we had better go by the book."

"Yes, I agree. We both are close to the family but I am sure that we'll be able to pull back and re-group, if necessary." Ronnie motioned to the guard to open the door and he said, "Attorney Spratt has been cleared to visit with Janita Morgan. Please take him to her holding area."

Jeff braced himself for what he was about to see as he followed the guard to the holding area where Janita had been placed for observation.

"Hi Janita."

Janita turned as she heard her Uncle Jeff's voice and tears begin to stream down her cheek.

"Please, go away. I don't want you or anyone else to see me in here."

Jeff now realized why his secretary had asked him if he thought that Janita would see him. Amy had done her homework and one of her police connections had obviously told her that Janita was not allowing anyone to visit with her. Jeff sighed and thought, "It's going to be difficult trying to reach this little girl."

"Janita, I need to talk with you for a few minutes. Will you look at me and talk to me?"

"I don't want to talk with anyone. Please, Uncle Jeff, go away."

"No, I will not." Looking at the prison guard, Jeff ordered, "Please, open the door."

As Jeff walked into the holding area, Janita stood with her back to him sobbing uncontrollably. Jeff looked at his best friend's daughter and he recalled how she had grown up with his daughter; how they had vacationed together and now to see her here was about to break his heart. Jeff moved toward Janita and she moved away. She was embarrassed to be seen in a place like this. She hurt so much and she just wanted the pain to go away. Jeff had to get to her and fast because he needed to be able to control this meeting.

"Janita, look at me."

Janita continued to stand with her back to him sobbing. Jeff repeated his stern order.

"Janita, look at me. Now!"

Slowly, she turned as the tears streamed down her cheeks and Jeff immediately hugged her.

"Little girl, you are in big trouble and I will need you to help me to get you out of this mess. Your family loves you and they will do whatever it takes to clear you. Honey, please trust me. Even though I am not your biological uncle, I consider myself a member of your family because your father and I have been best friends since we were kids. Our parents were best friends and since your birth you have been friends with my daughter. Now, please, Janita, stop crying and talk to me."

"Oh God, I hurt. I'm lonely. I'm embarrassed and I don't want to live anymore."

"*STOP IT! STOP IT! AND I MEAN IT!* Don't you ever say that again! Your family and I will not sit around and listen to this kind of talk. We know you are innocent and we will find out what happened. You will be freed and you will walk out of here. Compose yourself. Dry your tears. Sit down and talk with me."

With sputtering sobs, slowly, Janita began to wipe the tears from her cheeks. She sat down and for the first time since she was arrested she looked into the face of a loved one. Her uncle Jeff sat next to her and pulled out his personal digital assistant (PDA) with the tiny microphone and he explained to her that their conversation would be recorded, downloaded and later transcribed by Amy, his secretary.

"Janita, we have an issue that we must clarify before I can proceed with this interview. Janita Morgan, would you like for me to represent you, be your lawyer?"

Janita nodded her head, but Jeff said, "Honey, I need you to comment orally because this is being recorded and the gadget cannot record head nods."

"Yes, I would like for you to be my lawyer," Janita muttered.

"Thank you, I have a few other questions."

Janita interrupted, "Have you seen my sister, Julie or do you know how she is doing?"

"Yes, I did see her and Malcolm and they were both in pain but they were concerned and worried about you. Honey, you have to realize and understand that your entire family loves you and also your friends. Every one of us would like to help you. Janita, what do you remember about that night?"

"Nothing. I'm sorry, Uncle Jeff, but I honestly don't know what happened." Tears begin to re-appear in Janita's eyes.

"Take your time, baby."

As the tears flowed from Janita's eyes, she asked, "Can we meet later to discuss this? I will try to rethink that day and I'll give you whatever details I can recall."

7

Uncle Jeff put away his PDA, stood up, extended his arms and said, "Baby Girl, you look like you could use a hug." As Janita reluctantly took his hand, he hugged her and promised her that he would get her out of jail. Janita leaned her head on his shoulder and let out a sigh. Jeff motioned to the guard that he was ready to leave. The guard walked over and with the clicking noise of his keys, the door was opened. Jeff squeezed Janita's hand one more time and walked through the door without looking back because he was trying to hold back tears. As Jeff approached the front office he saw the Chief but decided to ignore him because he was in no condition to have a conversation with Ronnie. Ronnie called out to Jeff but Jeff only waved his hand to say good-bye.

Ronnie immediately realized how emotional and difficult the meeting must have been for Jeff. Ronnie thought, "I have known Jeff for twenty-five years and I've *never* seen tears in my friend's eyes." Ronnie walked into his office and as he sat quietly concentrating on the case, he decided to transfer the leadership duties of the Morgan case to his assistant. Ronnie pressed his intercom button and said "Isabella, locate Sergeant Chris Gude and schedule a meeting with him to discuss the Lee murder."

"Chief, Sergeant Gude is still on vacation. Should I have him located?"

"No. I can wait for his return."

By the time Jeff reached his car, he realized that he had not been successful at holding back his tears but he had avoided many of the policemen that normally ribbed him about "dressing and driving for success." Jeff sat in his car for a minute thinking about his friend, Joe, and the rest of the family and he whispered a silent prayer, "Lord, please ease their pain and please lead me and guide me with this case." Jeff looked at the clock and muttered, "I have exactly one hour until I meet with Joe. I must get my head together and I must be strong for my buddy." Slowly, Jeff pulled out from his parking space and decided to take a longer route back to the office by driving through City Park.

CHAPTER THREE

Joseph looked at his family and thought, 'the last time that I saw so much hurt on the faces of my children was on the sudden death of their mother, my beloved Jacquelyn. Jackie was so happy that morning. She was so excited about the financial report that she had received the night before regarding her new venture, The Tween Center. For many years, that center had been a dream of Jacquelyn's and it had finally become as successful as she had projected. What will happen to it now, he thought?' Following Jacquelyn's death, the Morgan family was thankful that Olivia Jenkins, Jacquelyn's friend and her first hire at the center had kept the center functioning until a family decision was made regarding its future.

Olivia believed in Jacquelyn's center and had volunteered her services for the first year. Later Jacquelyn paid Olivia $100 a week and they both had many laughs about feeling like millionaires when they had received a salary increase from zero dollars to $100 a week. When Janita assumed leadership of the center, she had to make many staffing changes but she could not nor did she want to lose Olivia. Janita often said that Olivia's presence ensured her Mother's spiritual presence in the business. And, now, Joseph thought, the Morgan family would again need Olivia to continue the operation of the Center until Janita returned to the business.

Joseph looked at the sad faces of his children and said, "I'd like for each of you to talk about your last conversation with

Janita prior to the murder and please tell every little detail, no matter how unimportant it may seem to you."

Junior said, "I'll start the discussion. Janita and I had lunch the day before the er, er...."

"Murder", Julia added.

"I'm sorry, Sis."

"Junior, stop apologizing. Family, I'm fine. I appreciate your concern but we need to finish this meeting. Junior, will you please continue?"

"I stopped by the center on Wednesday around lunch time and since neither of us had eaten and neither of us had a busy day, we decided to check out the new restaurant, GUMBOS. By the way, you all need to try it because the food is delicious. The owner is from New Orleans and..."

"Please, Junior, enough about the damn food, what did you all talk about?" Jeanette interrupted.

"What do you think? We talked about what she has constantly talked about since she started running the Center. She was happy about her success. She ribbed me about my love life and questioned me about the lucky lady of the month. I asked her about her dating and for a moment she got serious and said that now since the center was making money she would have time to selectively accept some of the advances from my Frat brothers. I inquired about their identity and she refused to tell me but she assured me that she would be careful. She smiled and said, "There are a few aggravating creeps that I know that I could never date, not even for a million dollars." I laughed and said, "Give me the million dollars and I would date the creep." She laughed out happily and said, "Big brother, I bet you would do anything for that almighty dollar." I said, "No, not for a dollar but for a million dollars, I may just try anything."

Joseph smiled as he urged his son to continue his story.

"We enjoyed the lunch, the conversation and our drive back to the center. I told Janita that I was proud of her and even though she thanked me, she credited Mother with the center's

11

success because she felt like Mother was still guiding her at the center. Did you all know that whenever she has to make a major decision, she goes into Mother's office, closes the door and has a conversation with our mom? I reminded her that the office was no longer Mother's office, but it was *her* office. However, she explained that she had not yet called it *her* office because Mother was still there guiding her. "In time," she said, "it *will* become my office but only after I have earned it" I did let her know that I understood where she was coming from and that I liked her thinking. She hugged me and gave me a kiss on the cheek and walked off to the building. That was the last time that I talked with her but excitedly, she left a message on my answering machine regarding the successful financial report that she had received and she ended the message with, "Big Brother, very soon, Mother's office will be my office." I did not call her back because I thought it was too late when I got home from one of those very, very late business meetings, if you know what I mean. Now, I wish that I had called her back because it may have been about the time of the murder."

When Julia heard the word murder, she began to weep and Junior lovingly comforted his sister.

Julie whispered, "I'm okay. Now, if Junior is finished, I'll now tell you about my last visit with Janita. Actually, she came over to my house on that day because she had left the center earlier than normal to purchase tickets to the ice-skating show at the Plaza. She had decided to take her godchild, my baby, Amber, to the show. After she purchased the tickets she brought them over because she wanted to see the excitement on Amber's face when she told her about the event."

Julie paused as she remembered the beautiful, happy face of her daughter as Janita pulled out the tickets. Julie continued, "When Janita told Amber that they also had dinner reservations before the show, Amber screamed with joy. Amber felt like a big girl and she begged her Nanny to let her spend the night with her. We all know how difficult it was for Janita to say no to Amber. I

12

asked Janita if she had made plans for the night and she laughed and said, "Yes, with Eric DaSalle tonight at nine." We both laughed and I said, "Girl, you know he's a dog because I'm also making plans to be with him tonight."

The startled Joseph looked at his daughters in disbelief and said, "Who in the hell is this Eric guy? Julie, are you having an affair?"

Junior, Jeanette and Julie all laughed at their pop and Julie continued, "No, Dad, I'm not having an affair. Eric DaSalle is the good looking...."

Jeanette shouted, "and sexy."

"...and sexy, African American doctor that stars on ED on Thursday nights."

Junior mumbled, "Pop, he ain't all that!"

"Okay, okay," Joseph replied, "Julie, please continue."

"Well, I did agree to allow Amber to spend the night. We decided to eat dinner together so we prepared steaks and salad. Amber began to pack the clothes and other junk that she wanted to take with her to Janita's house. I prepared the steaks, Janita prepared the salad and we decided not to waste time cooking the potatoes but would buy the ones on special at Clo's Hamburger Shop."

"Are the potatoes still on sale?"

"Yes, Junior, they are $ .99 with as many toppings as you would like. Janita went to Clo's Hamburger Shop while I set the table and made iced tea. She returned with the potatoes and we ate dinner. We cleaned the kitchen, but Janita did most of it because I had to repack Amber's clothes and remove some of trinkets that she had decided to take with her." Julie smiled as she said; "My child had packed so much that she wanted to take two pieces of luggage. It was really a delightful evening and I will always be thankful that it occurred. Nothing unusual happened. Janita was happy and enjoying the success of the Center."

"Pop, as I think back, the only disturbing part of the evening was Janita's anger at someone that she had seen at Clo's Hamburger Shop. I think he had worked for Mother at the center and Janita fired him after she assumed leadership. Janita made the statement, "The creep does not understand or he does not want to understand that I did not like him as an employee nor do I like him as a person." That creepy man had upset Janita and she shouted, 'The center is better off without him'."

Junior asked, "Julie, did Janita identify the dude?"

"When I questioned the identity of the creep, Amber entered the room and our attention turned to Amber. Janita and Amber selected two videos to take with them and they left. Oh, God, that was the last time that I saw my beautiful little girl alive. I miss her so much."

Joseph walked over to Julie and hugged his sobbing daughter and Junior suggested that perhaps the discussions should stop for a few minutes in order for Julie to have a break.

"No," Julie cried, "we must finish this before noon so that daddy will be prepared when he meets with Uncle Jeff."

"Pop," Jeanette said, "I hope that you are taping these discussions because I don't want Julie to have to go through this again until it is absolutely necessary."

"Yes, baby, I'm taping it."

Trying to hold back tears, Jeanette stared at her older sister, and she wondered how Julie would get through these difficult days. Jeanette knew Julie had to be in great pain because her only child was dead and her sister, who was also her best friend, was in jail for the murder. Wiping the tears from her eyes, Jeanette composed herself and continued the discussion.

"I may have been the last family member to talk with Amber and Janita that night. I had been in meetings all day and Janita had left several messages throughout the day for me so I called her as soon as I got home. That was about nine o'clock. Amber answered the telephone and of course, she had to tell me about the movie that she had been watching with her Nanny.

Janita took the phone from Amber and instructed Amber to go to bed. Amber kissed Janita goodnight and according to Janita that was the third goodnight kiss that she had received from Amber. Every time Amber got into her bed she would think of something to tell Janita and she would return to the living room and the goodnight activities would have to be re-started. Janita actually thought it was funny. I told her she was the aunt that was spoiling our baby. When I asked Janita about the urgent messages she had left for me during the day, she scolded me for not returning her calls earlier because the good news that she had wanted to share with me was now old news. Of course, you all know that her good news was the great financial report that she had received regarding the center. Janita was very happy but she was also a little tired, so she did not want to discuss business. She did, however, tell me about her dinner with Julie and about that creep that she had seen at Clo's Hamburger Shop. Janita tried to make me remember the guy because according to Janita the creep had flirted with me prior to Mother's death. I jokingly told her that the man was obviously, truly a creep and not my cup of tea because I could not remember him." Jeanette added, "Somehow, I can always remember good looking men but I could not and still can not even picture this dude. During our discussion about the creep, the door bell rang and when Janita looked through the peep hole, she said, 'Darn it, the creep is at my door, now what in the hell does he want?' I laughed and said, "Well Sis, I guess baby sitting can sometimes be used as a shield and a protection." She laughed as we said goodnight and hung up the phone. Jeanette pensively concluded, "Amber and Janita were both fine and happy at nine thirty that evening. I don't know what could have happened after we talked, but, I'm willing to bet that the creep will know what happened."

"Do any of you know the name of the creep?"

"No, Pop, I don't know him but why not ask Janita?" Joseph reminded his son that Janita had not been responding to any one since the incident but he was going to give the information that was being gathered to Jeff for follow-up on all details.

Jeanette added, "Olivia from the center will also be able to identify the creep."

Joseph said, "I am not sure if any of the details will help Jeff with the investigation, but I wanted to be prepared for our meeting this afternoon."

Julie asked, "Pop, did you speak with Janita on that day?"

"Yes baby, early in the morning when she had received her financial report from the accountant. However, we really did not spend time discussing the details because I was on my way to a meeting. I did, however, congratulate her and I promised to take her to dinner on the weekend. In fact, I told Janita that I would take all of you to dinner and she agreed to coordinate the outing."

Joseph glanced down at his watch. He thanked his children for sharing their information and offered to treat them to lunch. Without any hesitation, Junior accepted his father's offer by saying, "Thanks Pop, now pass me your plastic." The family laughed because Junior was always the first to accept a free meal.

Junior asked, "Pop, do we have a limit? I think I'll take my sisters to Gumbos, the new restaurant that I told you all about earlier?"

Daddy Morgan gave his credit card to Junior and said, "There is no limit, son, especially if you can cheer up my girls."

Julie and Jeanette kissed their father goodbye and as they left the house with Junior, Jeanette mumbled, "Junior, this food had better be good because my mouth is watering for the barbecue at the Rib Shack."

Joseph Morgan smiled at his children as he closed the door.

CHAPTER
FOUR

Joseph Morgan walked to his kitchen for a drink of water. As he sipped from the glass, he realized how tired he had become. He slowly walked into the den and as he looked out of the French doors, he noticed the old fashioned swing that hung between two of the pine trees in the back yard. Joseph smiled and walked outside.

Jacquelyn, his deceased wife, was so excited when she spotted the dilapidated swing hanging on its stand with one chain as they drove along one of the country roads on the outskirts of town. Jacquelyn insisted on stopping and asking the young couple to sell the swing to her. Those kids thought Jackie was crazy when she offered them $50.00 for the swing and they happily sold it to her. The young man was so grateful that he offered to clean it, repair it and deliver it to her. Jackie gave the money to the couple and she trusted them to keep their word about the fix-up and delivery of the swing. Joseph remembered how he teased his wife about kissing her $50 good-bye because he was convinced that the couple would not drive 50 miles into the city to deliver that old swing. Joseph recalled how Jacquelyn had scolded him about not trusting people. She accused him of being a member of the doubting Thomas fan club. Two days after the purchase of the swing, an old truck drove into the Morgan's driveway and to Joseph's amazement, the young man had restored the beauty of the antique swing and delivered it as promised. The young couple hung the swing exactly where Jacquelyn wanted it. When they had finished hanging it Jackie was so impressed that she gave the couple another $50 because she claimed it was fair. She had calculated that the cost, if done

17

---

in the city, would have been more. Jacquelyn often teased him as she claimed the extra $50 eliminated the need for her to nag and wait for the champion procrastinators, her husband and son, to redo the swing. Jacquelyn's swing became the favorite spot in the backyard landscape.

Joseph opened the French doors and walked out onto the covered patio. In deep thought, he slowly strolled over to Jacquelyn's swing. Sitting down, he whispered, "Oh, Jackie, I miss you so much." Joseph leaned back on the swing, closed his eyes and he could feel Jacquelyn's presence. Joseph thought about the loneliness and pain in his heart but as he looked upward the hurt was eased because he believed that his wife was in heaven looking down on her family.

Joseph's thoughts drifted to the day that Jacquelyn had died. When they awoke that morning, Jacquelyn asked if he would like to go to Mass with her. Joseph agreed to go to Mass but he would have to drive his car because of an early morning business appointment. The Morgans entered church together; they received communion together and following Mass they walked out of church together. Joseph then whispered to his wife, "I will need to leave now but pretty lady, can I walk you to your car?" Jacquelyn responded, "Thank you, my love, but I need to talk with a couple of people here before I leave." Joseph kissed his wife good-bye and he walked from the church to his car. Suddenly, Joseph felt a chill and a voice whisper, "Look back." Joseph slowly turned and looked back at his wife and as he did, Jacquelyn waved good-bye and blew a kiss to him. Joseph smiled and blew a return kiss to his wife and she moved her face as though she was catching the kiss on her cheek. Suddenly, Jacquelyn fell and Joseph ran back to the church, pushed his way through the crowd that had circled around. He knelt at her side and whispered "Jacquelyn, Jacquelyn." Jacquelyn did not respond. She was unconscious, but Joseph begged "Please, Jackie, wake up!" Someone said, "We called 911 and the ambulance is on the way." The priest knelt at

Jacquelyn's side and began to pray. Everything seemed to Joseph to be occurring so fast. Jackie would not wake up, the priest was praying and her friends who had attended Mass were crying.

Upon the arrival of the ambulance, the paramedics immediately begin to work on Jacquelyn and one of them said, "Sir, would you please move back for a minute."

Joseph realized that Jacquelyn had not moved since she had fallen and fearfully he began to cry.

"Mr. Morgan we are going to take your wife to the Emergency Department at Central Hospital. Will you be able to meet us there?"

Joseph said, "I would like to ride in the ambulance with my wife."

"Sir, I understand but I will need the space to treat your wife." The paramedic looked at Reverend Dean Bowman for assistance and the priest said, "Joseph, come with me, I'll drive you to the hospital." Joseph followed Father Bowman to his car and the two men drove to the hospital in total silence but with prayers in their hearts and in their minds.

Upon their arrival to the hospital, Father Bowman questioned the location of Jacquelyn Morgan. The nurse asked them to have a seat and she would check with the physician. Joseph could not sit down; he wanted to see his wife. Shortly, the nurse returned to the waiting area and she asked Mr. Morgan to please follow her but when he entered the room, Jacquelyn was not there. In fact, it was a meditation room with the doctor standing waiting for them to enter. No, Joseph thought, this is not happening but the doctor interrupted his thoughts.

"Good morning Mr. Morgan, I'm Dr. Webber. I'm so sorry but Mrs. Morgan didn't make it."

"Oh, no, oh, no, not my beautiful Jacquelyn."

"Sir, there was nothing that we could do, she was dead on arrival. I am sorry."

The priest tried to comfort Joseph and Joseph whispered, "I want to see her." The nurse said, "Yes, sir, you may see her, will you come with me." She looked at the priest and asked, "Do you know how to locate other members of the family." Father Bowman nodded and walked over to the telephone and called his secretary and asked her to locate the Morgan children. The secretary told him that everyone had been notified and all were on their way to the hospital.

Joseph walked into the emergency treatment room and looked at his wife who seemed to be asleep with a beautiful smile on her face. He could not believe that she was dead, and that she had left him, alone, on this earth. Joseph had always thought that he would die before Jacquelyn. They had had so many plans and dreams to fulfill before one of them would die. Joseph slowly walked over to the gurney and as he cried he leaned over, held his beautiful wife in his arms. Then he kissed her soft lips and whispered, "Honey, I will always love you."

As Joseph walked out of the treatment room, he asked, "Have you been able to locate the children?"

"Yes, they had been contacted and should be arriving soon. Joseph, I told the nurse that we would be in the meditation room. I asked her to please escort the children to that room, so let's go there to wait for them."

Joseph shook his head and the priest led him to the waiting area.

Later, as Joseph sat in silence and as the priest knelt in prayer, the door to the mediation room slowly opened. Father Bowman immediately rushed toward the door to meet the four Morgan children.

Looking around the room, Junior whispered, "Daddy, where is Mother?"

The siblings could all see that their father had been crying. Nervously Janita questioned, "Daddy, is Mother sick?"

Jeanette, the youngest daughter ran to her father and sobbed, "Daddy, where is my Mother?"

Joseph stood up and looking at his family, he whispered, "Children, I'm sorry that I have to tell you this, but Mother is dead."

Jeanette screamed and Junior shouted, "Pop, what happened and where is my Mother?"

Father Bowman said, "Your mother died suddenly at church this morning. We don't know what caused it."

The nurse who had escorted the children to the meditation room told them that they could see their mother and she would take them to the treatment room. Father Bowman walked with the children to the treatment room as Joseph sat alone, Doctor Webber returned to the room and explained that since Jacquelyn's death was sudden they would like to perform an autopsy on her. Joseph's first thought was to say he did not want them to cut on his beautiful wife. The doctor explained the autopsy findings could help identify problems that might be hereditary. Dr. Webber also explained that the sudden death was classified as a coroner's case and that if they did not do the autopsy at Central Hospital, the coroner would perform the autopsy without consent. Joseph signed the autopsy form and after the physician left the meditation area, Joseph sat alone in silence until he heard the door open.

"Grandfather, where is my mommy?"

Joseph looked up and Malcolm, Julie's husband entered the room with Amber, the first and only grandchild of Joseph and Jacquelyn Morgan. Malcolm looked at his father-in-law in disbelief and watched as Joseph placed Amber on his knee.

"Amber, I need to tell you something very important but first I am going to have your father go to the nurse's station to find your mommy for us."

Malcolm rushed out of the room to the nurse's station, and he was taken to the treatment room where Jacquelyn had been pronounced dead. As Malcolm entered the room, Julie ran to him in tears and questioned, "Where is Amber?"

"She's with Joe. My God, baby, what happened?"

21

"I don't know, honey, but we need to go to Amber and try to explain this to her."

As Julie and Malcolm opened the door to the meditation room, they heard their daughter say, "Grandfather, is my grandmother in heaven."

The startled Joseph said, "Yes baby, but how did you know?"

"My grandmother told me that one day you would be very sad and she would not be with you because she would be in heaven. She wanted me to be a big girl and to tell you that she loves us all very much. Grandfather, today you are very sad, but my grandmother still loves you."

Julie walked over and hugged Amber. Malcolm lifted her from Joseph's knee. Trying to hold back tears, Joseph leaned over, kissed his granddaughter and walked out of the room to be with his children and to once again say good-bye to his precious wife. As Joseph entered the room, he hugged his four children and they moved back for him to be with their mother. Junior leaned and kissed his mother good-bye and he ushered his three sisters out of the room. Joseph looked at Jacquelyn; his beloved wife and the only woman that he had ever dated and had ever loved. He stood alone; he reached down and lifted her left arm then kissed her left hand. He kissed the wedding ring that he had placed on her ring finger thirty-five years earlier. As Joseph held her hand, he sat next to his wife, and he held her in his arms. He looked at her wedding rings; the rings that she had claimed delayed their marriage because she thought he had paid too much for them. He smiled as he remembered the first time that he had seen the rings. They were beautiful and he immediately knew that he wanted them for Jacquelyn, no matter the cost. He again kissed her rings and he recalled one of their conversations regarding death. "Honey," she said, "I love my wedding rings and I don't want them stolen from my fingers after my death nor do I want to be buried with them. So, if I should die before you, will you please remove them from my finger and give them to one of the children?" Joseph sobbed almost uncontrollably then he slid the rings from her finger and slipped them into his pants pocket. Joseph kissed his Jacquelyn for the last time and he walked out of the room to join the family.

As Joseph approached, Julie asked, "Amber, would you like to say goodbye to your grandmother?"

"No," Amber replied, "because she's already in heaven looking down at us."

Junior picked up his niece and said, "Amber, I think we could learn something from you."

Amber then looked at her uncle and asked, "Like what?"

Malcolm took his daughter from Junior's arms and said, "I'm going to take Amber with me but I'll meet you later at Joe's house."

Goodbye kisses were exchanged and Amber and Malcolm left the hospital.

Following the completion of all of the hospital forms, Father Bowman asked the family if he could drive them home. Junior said, "Thank you, but I have my car." Father Bowman said, "Joseph, if you would like to give me your keys, I can have your cars delivered to your home later." Joseph said, "Thank you. You can have my car delivered, but I'll come for Jacquelyn's car."

The Morgan family left the hospital together in Junior's car and all of them wanted to go to their parent's home. During the ride home, Julie asked, "Daddy, I'm a little confused about Amber's comments regarding Mom's death. Was Mom sick?"

"Your mother told me that Amber had questioned her regarding death when Malcolm's father died and her Grandmother Lorraine was very sad. Jacqueline explained to Amber how married people mourn the death of a spouse and I see that Amber remembered the conversation." The family continued their ride home in silence, however, as they neared their house, they noticed many of the church parishioners had gathered in the yard awaiting their arrival.

23

"Pop," Junior said, "please send them away."

As they exited the car, Joseph looked at the crowd and said, "By now, you all must know that Jacquelyn died this morning immediately following Mass and she's now, as my granddaughter said, in heaven looking down on all of us. We thank you all for meeting us here because we know that you are here to help us. As soon as we have made plans I assure you that we will contact many of you for your assistance. In the meantime, pray for us."

Joseph unlocked his front door, led his family into his house and closed the door so that he could be alone with his children.

Later, the children commented on how well their father had handled the crowd and how proud they were of him. However, Joseph believed that Jacquelyn must have whispered those words into his ears because she had a special skill at communicating with their church friends. The parishioners loved Jacquelyn and Jacquelyn loved her church. It was comforting to know that she had died following Mass at her beloved church. Jacquelyn died happy. Joseph often said that he would always remember the wave and the smile that she gave to him just before she died, and that beautiful vision would remain with him until his death.

Joseph relaxed in Jacquelyn's swing, and he concentrated on the vision of his wife's last moments. Suddenly, the ring of the telephone interrupted his thoughts. It was Melrose Clark, his secretary, calling to remind him that it was time for him to be leaving his home for his appointment with Attorney Spratt. Joseph thanked her for the call and told her he would call her immediately following that meeting. Melrose also reminded him that lunch would be delivered. Joseph once again thanked Melrose, picked up his attaché case, walked out to his car and drove off to his friend's office.

CHAPTER FIVE

The Morgan siblings walked into Gumbos and Jeanette said, "Junior, you know that I could be enjoying barbecue right now so this food had better be good."

Junior smiled and said, "I am sure that you will enjoy the food. The Mardi Gras decoration is great and I believe it will be a refreshing change, especially after that session with Pop. Julie, if you think that this restaurant is too much for you, please let me know."

"Oh, no, I'm fine. In fact, at this time, I would rather be here than at home with Malcolm. He is hurting and he misses Amber so much. Malcolm is upset with me and is not treating me very well because he can't understand how I can try to help defend Janita when our daughter is dead. I have tried to explain to him that Janita loved Amber too much to hurt her. I asked him to wait until a thorough investigation has been completed before we turn our back on a sister who has always been there for us. Many times, Janita has bailed him out financially with all of the harebrain ideas that he has had to make money. For the first time in her life, Janita needs us and now he wants me to turn my back on her." Julie looked at her brother and she said, "I can't do that and I will not do that."

Junior hugged his sister. Jeanette held her hand and said, "Sis, I'm here for you and you have my door key. Please, stay at my place whenever you need an escape pad."

"Now, Julie, you know that my doors are also open but you also know that my place may not always be clean."

The sisters laughed and Julie said, "No thank you, sir, I really don't want to pick up any diseases from your place."

25

"Junior, why don't you get maid service to clean that filthy ass house."

Julie said, "Let's not talk about that dirty place right now because it may spoil my appetite."

"Jeanette, you're right. I'll do it. Will you please make the arrangement with the service?"

"That's a deal, now, let's try this delicious looking food that our big Bro is introducing us to."

"Yes, let's eat and I promise you that you will like it."

CHAPTER
SIX

At exactly one o'clock Joseph Morgan walked into Attorney Spratt's office, and said, "Hi, Amy, I'm sure that Jeff's awaiting my arrival."

"Yes, sir, he is."

As Joseph opened the door, his long time friend, Jeff, was standing looking out of the window in deep thought. Jeff turned as the door opened and he walked over to Joseph and gave him a handshake and a hug.

"My friend, we have big problems and we need your help."

"Yes, I know and I have already agreed to take Janita's case."

"Jeff, I knew that I could count on you, but what do you mean, that you have agreed to take the case; when, where, how and with whom?"

"I met with Janita this morning."

"Did she talk with you?"

"Yes, she did but I must admit the first part of our meeting was spent trying to convince her to help herself. She's hurting and is very concerned about the family."

"Did she remember anything about Friday night?"

"No, but I did ask her to take her time and try to remember any little detail that had occurred and to be prepared to discuss it with me during our next visit."

Amy opened the door and announced that lunch had been delivered. The deliveryman set out the food and Amy signed the check for the bill and the tip.

The two friends sat down to eat and Jeff said, "I've asked Paul Mason, a private investigator, to join this meeting in about

27

an hour because I'm sure that we'll need to use him during this investigation."

"Jeff, before we start, will you please tell me about your meeting with Janita."

"It was very emotional and she wasn't able to share any information with me. I'll see her again in the morning; hopefully by then she may remember something about that night. Joe, you do realize that if Janita had shared information with me, I wouldn't have been able to discuss the details with you. I'm Janita's lawyer and regardless of my friendship with you, I'll treat your daughter's case with the same confidentiality that all of my clients receive. Buddy, do you understand what I'm saying?"

Joseph looked at Jeff as though he was staring through his friend and slowly he shook his head and said, "I do understand."

Jeff watched as his friend attempted to hold back his tears. Joseph composed himself, looked up and said, "I met with the children today and they outlined their last conversations with Janita. We taped it for you in order to eliminate the need to repeat the questions. We're all concerned about Julie because she's hurting so much."

Jeff looked up and said, "Joe, I'm sorry for failing to inquire about Julie's condition. I overlooked the fact that the victim and the accused are both from the same family. How are Julie and Malcolm?"

"She's really very delicate right now and her marriage may not survive this crisis. Perhaps we are expecting too much from Malcolm but we don't know how we would react if we were in his shoes. I had hoped that he would try to understand that we are family and we are all working to solve this case." Joseph paused as he thought about his daughter and her husband. Then, he opened his attaché case and removed two tapes of that morning's meeting. He paraphrased the discussions, then handed the tapes to Jeff.

"Thanks, Joseph, for the tapes. I'm sure that this was difficult for all of you. I'll keep the originals but I'll have Amy get a copy made for Paul's review."

Jeff labeled the two tapes *Original* and he buzzed for Amy so that she could have the tapes copied before his next appointment with Paul. After Jeff explained to Amy what he needed, Amy questioned, "Are you ready for me to have your lunch trays removed?" Jeff said, "Yes, and please call Melrose to let her know that she did make a great lunch selection." "Will do," Amy said as she left Jeff's office.

Joseph said, "Jeff, there's one thing on the tapes that has been on my mind since the meeting. It may not be important, but in Julie and Jeanette's last conversation with Janita, she spoke of a former employee of the Center that she had recently encountered and both times Janita called the young man the Creep. None of the girls could remember the young man but Janita didn't like him. I could contact Olivia at the center and perhaps she'll remember the former employee but I wanted to discuss it with you first. Should I do further investigation?"

"Paul Mason will follow-up and will investigate every aspect of this case but thank you for the tapes because this will eliminate our need to talk with Julie." Jeff looked at his friend and said, "Joe, I'm going to ask you to trust me with your daughter's case and I'm going to ask you to concentrate on your family, especially Julie. They need you now, more than ever. You'll need to be strong for them. Are you okay with this request?"

"Of course, I'm okay with your request, and you are doing exactly what I expected of you. Jeff, you're the brother that I never had and I trust you with my life. Now, my friend, take care of my daughter."

Jeff nodded in agreement. "I don't know if we can get Janita out on bail, but I'm sure that we won't have any problems raising bail because of the real estate that we own. Do you agree?"

"Yes, yes, of course."

"Joe, this case will also be difficult for Ronnie. To ward off any accusations of favoritism, I do expect Ronnie to go by the book, but we'll need to understand his position. You'll need to discuss this with your family because it may be difficult for them to understand Ronnie's comments and actions. Ronnie has been friends with us too many years to be torn apart now. We'll need to understand and to tolerate each other. I'll talk with Ronnie and let him know that we do understand the position that he's in. You know, Ronnie may remove himself from the investigation but I would prefer that he not do that."

"Why not?"

"Well, it would probably be better to have a friend investigate rather than someone trying to make a name for him or herself. I hope that Ronnie doesn't make a change before I talk with him."

At exactly two thirty there was a tap on the door and Jeff said to Joseph, "That will be Paul Mason. I told Amy to send him in as soon as he arrived. Are we ready for him or do we have more to discuss?"

"No, I'm done but friend, this is your case and you make the decisions."

Jeff smiled as he patted Joe on the back and said, "Thanks, pal." Jeff walked to his office door, opened it and said, "Come in Paul." As Paul entered, Jeff said, "Paul, this is Joseph Morgan, the father of my client, Janita Morgan." The two men shook hands as Jeff said, "Paul, Joe and I were about to end our meeting, do you have any questions for him?"

"Yes, only one thing, Mr. Morgan; will you or your family prepare a list of Janita's friends, male and female for me? We may have to question them, later."

"Okay, I can do that. Is there anything else that you may need from me?"

"Not now, but I'll contact Jeff if additional information is needed. Oh, yes, you can give your list to Jeff, he will be our liaison."

Jeff said, "Thanks, Joe, for the information, I'll be in touch very soon."

Joseph shook Paul's hand and Jeff walked to the door with his friend and said good-bye. Jeff closed the door, looked at Paul with a confused expression, and said, "What in the hell was that about? Since when have you started using me as a liaison? Why are you handling this case different than our other cases and why are you asking Joe for a list of Janita's friends? Why, Paul, Why?"

Paul looked at Jeff and said, "Sir, you are paying me to do a job, so I'm hoping that you will trust me because you know that every great investigator has reasons for making requests."

"So, you have heard something, haven't you?"

"Well, Sir...."

Stop calling me Sir," Jeff shouted. "My name is Jeff, Jeff Spratt. Okay. Please, just call me Jeff."

"Yes, Sir, oh-er-I'm sorry, I mean Jeff." I've heard gossip but I will not discuss it with you until I have investigated the details."

"I understand." Jeff walked over to his desk and said, "Paul, Joseph and his family had discussions regarding their last meeting with Janita and each of their statements were taped. Amy made a copy for your review in hopes that you'll not have to question the Morgan family, especially the victim's mother."

"What a great idea! Did you request this?"

"Oh, no that's how Joseph Morgan operates, especially when he wants a problem to be rapidly solved."

"Jeff, I understand that you and Mr. Morgan were infant friends, so, I need to know if I'll be restricted with this investigation?"

"Of course not, I'm expecting your best."

31

"Great, I'll be in touch when I have information to share with you." Jeff walked with Paul to the door. They shook hands and Paul walked out of the door.

Jeff closed the door and leaning against it, thought. "Wow, I wonder what is being said out in the community." Jeff knew that people would not gossip with him about the Morgans but he was very curious and wondered what Paul was hearing. Jeff walked over to his credenza and poured a glass of water and was drinking it when Amy tapped on the door and without hesitating she immediately opened the door.

"Jeff, do you have anything else that I need to do before I go home for today?"

"I don't think so, thanks."

"Well, if you need me, I'll be at home or on the beeper. Here's your schedule for tomorrow. Please remember that you'll need to be in court for ten o'clock and the case folders are on your desk. Have a good evening, Jeff."

"Thanks, Amy. Good night."

Just as Amy was about to close the office door, Jeff said, "Amy, wait. Please sit down for a few minutes, I need to discuss something with you. I know that you're active in the community and I also know that you're aware of most of the activities that are hot topics. What have you heard about the Morgan case?"

Amy looked at her boss with a quizzical expression.

"Amy, I know that you despise gossip and I know that you're aware of my relationship with the Morgan family, but Paul heard something that he's not prepared to share with me, yet. Do you have any idea what he could be shielding from me until it is confirmed?"

Amy bit her bottom lip, closed her eyes then looked up at him. "Jeff, there may be questions about Janita's sexual orientation." Jeff's mouth dropped open.

"Good-bye boss. Have a good evening."

CHAPTER SEVEN

Joseph was sitting home alone in his den looking at the evening local news when the ring of the telephone startled him.

"Good evening," the baritone voice warmly greeted the caller.

"Pop, I'm returning your call," the exhausted caller replied.

"Hi Jeanette. Thanks for returning my call. The private investigator that's working on Janita's case with Uncle Jeff has asked that we prepare a list of all of Janita's male and female friends. Baby, will you handle this for me?"

"Sure, I will, but why don't they ask Janita, or use her address book that was removed from her house?"

"I don't know, baby girl, but I think that we should do what they ask of us."

"Pop, you're right. I'll drop the list off at your place after work tomorrow."

"Thanks, baby," the weary Joseph replied.

"Pop, are you okay?"

"Yes, honey, I'm fine, I'm just a little tired. This has been a very full day."

"Have you eaten anything, yet?"

"No, but I'll find something later."

"Sit tight, old man, I'll be there shortly with something delicious for you to eat."

"Baby, that won't be necessary."

"Pop, I know that it's not necessary but I'll see you in a little bit."

Jeanette hung up the phone, pulled the menu for Gumbo's from her purse, called in an order for her father, and decided to add a salad for herself. She looked at Buttons, her black and white cocker spaniel and said, "I'm sorry, pretty baby. I know that you're tired of being alone, but I'm a little concerned about your grandfather. I don't have time to walk with you, right now, but while I'm gone you can play in the back yard." She gave Buttons a playful hug, opened the patio door and Buttons ran outside.

Jeanette picked up her order at Gumbo's and in less than thirty minutes she was opening the door of her father's home. Joseph was sitting in his recliner dozing and as she glanced at him, she realized that he had aged tremendously in just a few days. Jeanette walked over and kissed his forehead.

"Hi, baby, I guess I dozed off."

"Yes, you did but that's okay because you needed the rest."

Jeanette walked to the kitchen to serve the food. Joseph followed her and watched as she washed her hands. Observing her, he said, "Baby Girl, you're so much like your mother; your hair, your facial features, your voice, your mannerisms, your complexion, your size and on some occasions, very few occasions, you can even be as sweet as Jacquelyn."

"Thanks for the compliment," Jeanette replied as she set the table and poured two small glasses of wine.

"Come Pop, let's eat."

As Joseph moved closer to the table, he noticed the bag on the countertop was from Gumbo's.

"I guess Junior was correct when he raved about that new restaurant," Joseph said smiling.

"Pop, the food was delicious and it'll remind you of Grandmother's cooking. Now, sit down tired, hungry old man and let's enjoy this time together."

"Okay, okay, my precious child."

34

"Yes, I know that I'm your precious child tonight because I'm feeding you. I think I'll wait until tomorrow and see if you still think that I'm precious."

They both laughed as they sat down to eat.

CHAPTER EIGHT

As Jeff picked up the ringing phone, he glanced at the clock and he wondered why Amy would be calling him at seven in the morning.

"Good morning Amy."

"Hi, boss, your contact at the station said bail will probably be set at $250,000 for Janita Morgan and her arraignment is scheduled for nine o'clock. I've asked your friends to schedule Janita first so that you can make your ten o'clock court schedule."

"Thanks Amy, you're a jewel. I don't know what I'd do without you running my life. I do appreciate all that you do for me."

"Yes, I know you appreciate me and that's why my income is just above the poverty level."

"Oh, yeah, if that's the case, we need to contact the accountant because something is wrong with our books. Someone else has been receiving your money, my friend. I'll see you later."

"Jeff, wait," Amy shouted. "If things are running behind schedule when you call me what should I do about your ten o'clock court appearance?"

"Ohoooooo, let's see. I'll call and alert Bubba to meet my client and start off for me."

"Jeff, who in the hell is Bubba?"

"You know, the last kid that did a practice rotation with us."

"Jeff, the *man's* name is Jeremy and that kid is thirty three years old."

"Well, he looks like Bubba," Jeff muttered.

"Good-bye boss," Amy said as she laughed and hung up the phone.

Jeff looked at the clock and thought, I don't have much time before nine o'clock so I'll need to speed it up.

Jeff arrived at the jail at seven forty and announced that he needed to see his client, Janita Morgan, before her arraignment. The front desk officer buzzed lockup and said, "Tell cell 433 that her lawyer is on his way downstairs." By the time Jeff reached the meeting room, Janita had been escorted to the area and was waiting for him. Janita smiled as Jeff approached her.

"Good morning," they both said simultaneously and they hugged.

Jeff informed his client that the meeting would be brief but he wanted to explain to her what would be happening that morning at her arraignment.

"Janita, this will probably be hard on you because you will be handcuffed and possibly shackled when you go into court. You'll be asked, how do you plea, and you will say, not guilty. Bail will be set at about $250,000 or above and it'll be up to us to post bail so that you will be allowed to go home. Are you ready to face the family?"

"No, " Janita thoughtfully responded. "I don't want that right now, plus I don't want the family worrying about bail."

"Janita, your family has the cash to post bail. You also have extensive property; therefore, we will not have a problem posting bail. Your only concern should be your return to your family and that could happen by late afternoon."

Janita walked away in deep thought, then slowly she questioned, "Can you delay posting bail?"

"Of course, but you know your father will want you home today, or as soon as possible. Until that happens he'll pressure me to speed up the bail process."

"Yes, I realize that but I can't face the family just yet, especially Julie and Malcolm."

Understanding Janita's predicament, Attorney Spratt questioned, "Are you requesting a delay in posting bail because if you are, your father will have to accept your decision."

"That's exactly what I'm requesting. I don't want my family to see me this morning in handcuffs and ankle shackles. It will hurt my father too much to see me looking like a criminal. I don't want him to know about the arraignment scheduled for this morning."

"Wait a minute, Janita. You're really putting me in an awkward position because I cannot lie to Joseph and I will not lie to him."

Janita slowly turned and looked directly into Attorney Jeff Spratt eyes and said, "I'm hiring you as my attorney and I plan to pay you for your services. I'll expect you to keep my case confidential or I'll have you disbarred."

"Well, Ms Morgan, welcome back," said the startled Attorney Spratt. "Now, you're sounding like the demanding little lady that you were prior to this crisis. I'll do as I've been instructed because I don't want to be disbarred. Now, do you plan to write a check or put the bill on a charge card because with this type of case I do expect one half of my $50,000 fee before the arraignment? Okay, Ms Disbarment Queen. I'll see you at nine."

Jeff motioned to the policeman to open the door so that he could leave. As Jeff walked away, he turned to look back at Janita and he smiled, as she stood with her mouth still open, motionless in shock regarding his legal fee.

Following his meeting with Janita, Jeff decided to see if Chief Ronnie Petit had arrived to work and whether he would have a few minutes to meet with him. As Jeff entered the front office, he noticed his buddy, Ronnie, walking from his car to the office with a small, brown paper lunch bag. Jeff quietly chuckled, shook his head and mused, it's true what they say, "You can take the boy from the country but you can't take the country out of the boy."

"Good morning Jeff, early start, huh."

"Yes," Jeff said and he followed Ronnie into the office. "Ron, who's in charge of the investigation of the Morgan case?"

"I had thought that I may be too close to the subjects and I had decided to assign it to my assistant, Chris Gude, but my wife thinks that's a bad idea."

"I agree with your wife. We really need someone who will be thorough but fair. Someone who will allow the evidence to determine the outcome rather than someone trying to look good in the community or even worse, someone trying to get your job. Ron, I'll never take advantage of our friendship and I'll never allow you to jeopardize your future because of this investigation."

"I know that." Ronnie replied. "I'll let you know later who our investigator will be. I may just keep it and let the little military guy do my leg work."

Jeff stood up, shook Ronnie's hand and said, "Thanks, man, I'll see you later."

Jeff walked to his car concentrating on Janita's comments regarding bail and not wanting to see her family. He understood Janita's feeling and he thought, if I were she, I would probably be doing the same thing. He noticed the time and decided to review his notes prior to the court case. He thought that if he went down to court early, he could review his notes in the courtroom and avoid calls from Joseph regarding Janita's case. Jeff also decided to turn off his cell phone, but all of these precautions made Jeff uncomfortable as though he was trying to deceive a friend. Jeff started the engine of his car and was about to pull out of his parking space, when suddenly, he stopped the engine, picked up his cellular phone and dialed the Chief's private cell phone.

"Ronnie, it's really important that I speak with Janita for a quick minute, can you have her contact me ASAP."

"Sure," Ronnie answered, "but it may be better for me to arrange that now, so please hold on for a minute."

"Franklin," Ronnie shouted, "Morgan's lawyer would like to speak with her; will you walk this phone down to her?"

Jeff could hear Ronnie speaking with his officer and he also heard Franklin shout for Janita.

"Janita, Janita Morgan, your lawyer is on the phone."

Janita walked to the bars, reached for the phone and immediately she and Franklin recognized each other.

"My God," Franklin said, "It's you. I didn't realize that you were the Janita Morgan in here."

Jeff could hear the conversation and he became relieved when he learned that Janita had obviously recognized an old friend that would be near her and could be available to watch over her.

"Hello."

"Hello, this is your Uncle Jeff, your hired lawyer and I have a question."

"Yes, my uncle, my lawyer, please ask your question."

"I understand why you do not want your father at the arraignment this morning, but will you allow him to visit with you later today? Janita, I'm a father and I need for you to understand that the parent is also hurting when their child is hurting. Baby, he needs to see you, he needs to see for himself that you're okay or he will continue to hurt. Please think about what I'm asking of you and give me an answer when I see you."

"I really don't have to think about it because at this time, I really need to see him. In fact, I'll call him and ask him to come to see me this afternoon. Thanks, Uncle Jeff, you are truly a good friend to my father and my family. I guess I'm beginning to believe that you are a pretty good lawyer and may be worth the $50,000 that I'll owe you. By the way, please ask Junior to withdraw $25,000 from my account so that I can make my first payment."

"Well, after all of these years, are you now beginning to believe that I'm a good, no, I mean a great lawyer. Little girl, you had better believe all of the things that you read about me in the newspaper. Yes, baby, I'm good and no, I will not give your message to Junior. You'll be indebted to me. See you at nine."

Janita handed the phone to Franklin.

"I may be back down later."

"It has been a long time. How are you and where have you been since college?"

"I decided to go into the airforce. Now I'm out and I'm home to stay. Listen, I need to take the phone back to the Chief but I'll see you later."

"Okay," Janita said and as Franklin began to walk away, she said, "Wait a minute. Will you please let me use the phone to call and leave a message for my father who's probably at Mass?"

Franklin looked behind him and while handing her the phone he said, "Make it fast."

Janita dialed her father's phone number and she was happy that he was not at home to answer the phone. Softly she said, "Good morning, Pop, this is Janita, I'm fine and I'm calling to ask you if you would come to visit with me today during visiting hours between, er,er...."

"Between two and three."

"Between two and three. I love you Pop."

Janita thanked Franklin for the use of the phone and Franklin turned to walk away.

"For your information, I'm not guilty."

"I believe you," Franklin said.

As Janita sat down she thought, "That's the first time that I said, I'm not guilty. My heart has been telling me that I couldn't harm anyone especially my precious niece. However, I can't remember what happened that night and I must remember in order to prove that I'm not guilty." Janita closed her eyes and thought, "God, I don't understand why I'm not able to remember what happened on Friday night. I have never had a problem like this in the past." Janita whispered, "I have got to remember, God, I have got to remember."

Franklin went directly to the Chief's office to return his cellular phone.

"Sir, I know prisoner Morgan. In fact, I was madly but secretly in love with her in high school. Of course, she didn't notice me because I was considered a nerd. She was so gorgeous and so smart."

The Chief looked up and said, "Franklin, I have a personal request. Please, don't call her prisoner to me. Her name is Janita, Janita Morgan. Her father has been my friend for twenty-five years, and it hurts for me to have her called prisoner. It's still too new for me to accept."

"Sir, I understand and for your information, she told me that she's not guilty and I do believe her."

"Oh", the Chief said, "is she talking now?"

"Yes, sir, she was in a pretty good mood."

"That's good news, Franklin, that is very good news. Franklin, buzz me about eight forty five so that we can move Janita down to the court house for her arraignment."

"Yes, Sir," Franklin replied and he closed the office door behind him as he left the Chief's office.

As the Chief sat down at his desk he muttered, "Yes, our girl is back and it seems as though she's going to help us." Ronnie opened the Janita Morgan file that had been placed on his desk and began to review the notes and reports that had been gathered on the case. Ronnie reviewed the list of items confiscated from Janita's home and the three glasses located on the cocktail table got his attention. He wondered who had used the third glass and he picked up a red pen and in the left margin he noted: identify three users for drinking glasses. Ronnie continued to read and add his notes and questions to the investigation reports.

In deep thought, the ringing of his cell phone startled Ronnie, but he located the phone in his shirt pocket and answered, "Petit."

"Ronnie, this is Jeff. Sorry to interrupt you again but if Joe calls please don't take his call until after the arraignment. Janita doesn't want him to see her in shackles and handcuffs so she doesn't want him to know about the hearing this morning."

"Do you really think that you can keep this from the entire Morgan family?"

"I don't know, but my client has ordered me not to tell her father so I won't. I can't stop everyone else."

"Good luck, man."

Ronnie hung up the phone, walked to the door, opened it and shouted, "Franklin, come in here."

"Yes, sir, Chief."

"Did Mr. Morgan call this morning?"

"Yes, sir, he did, but when I looked into your office you were on the telephone so I asked if he wanted to leave a message. He asked me to tell Janita that he would be here this afternoon for visiting hours. He also asked me if I had seen her and if I could tell him how was she doing. I told him she was in a good mood this morning and I let him know that I had gone to high school with Janita. He asked me to watch over her."

"Franklin, I hope you didn't tell him about the arraignment this morning."

"Oh, no sir, I wouldn't do that because I overheard Janita tell her attorney that she didn't want her family to see her in shackles."

"Franklin, you're a good man but you're not suppose to be listening to the attorney/client discussions."

"Yes, Sir, I know and I wouldn't have repeated what I overheard to you had you not questioned me regarding Mr. Morgan's knowledge of Janita's hearing. Sir, I'll never repeat that again."

"Franklin, when its time to leave, please drive my car to the back and I'll walk Janita to the car so that we can transfer her to the courthouse. I know that I'm going to be criticized and accused of giving Janita special treatment but I'll respond to those accusations later."

At eight forty, the Chief picked up his gun and holster and placed it around his waist. He glanced at his watch and walked out of his office to Janita's cell.

"Good morning, Janita Morgan. I understand from Franklin that you're having a better day today than you had yesterday."

"Hi, Uncle Ronnie. I'm better because I know that I didn't kill Amber. I loved her too much to harm her. I'm not sure what happened yet but I will remember. I will remember."

"I believe you, honey, and I'm committed to finding out what happened so that we can get you back home very soon. Janita, we have to leave now and I'll have to handcuff you."

"I know you do, but do you have to put those things around my ankles?"

"We are going out of the back door from here so I'll have Franklin place the shackles around your ankles when we reach the court house."

"Is he married?"

"Is who married?"

"George Franklin."

"I don't think so. Are you interested in that young man?"

"No, I'm just curious about an old classmate."

"Sure, you're just curious about an old classmate, just as he is curious about you, an old classmate."

"Are you saying that George asked about me?"

"Yes, he did. Okay, Janita, the car is out back, let's go."

Janita was rushed out of the door and into the Chief's car.

44

CHAPTER
NINE

Attorney Jeff Spratt had been working at the defendant's table for about thirty minutes when he heard the court reporter and the clerk enter the courtroom. Jeff decided to quickly check to see if he had received any e-mail from Amy. He immediately replied "yes" to her request for him to meet with Paul that afternoon. Jeff whispered, "I certainly hope Paul has additional information to exonerate Janita."

As Jeff cleared the table of his personal items, he glanced behind him and was surprised at the number of people who had entered the room. Through the crowd, Jeff was shocked to see Joseph Morgan, Junior. He walked toward Junior and the two men shook hands.

"Surprised to see you here. How did you find out?"

"The DA mentioned it to Julie this morning and she assumed that you did not want Pop to know so she called me."

"Correction, please. My client did not want me to tell her father. She did not want her family to see her in the shackles and handcuffs."

The side door of the courtroom abruptly opened and Ronnie walked in with Janita. He immediately sat her at the table before any of the reporters had noticed her entrance. Junior rushed over to his sister and they embraced with neither of them saying a word but both had teary eyes.

"Janita, please take your seat," Ronnie softly whispered.

"We love you," Junior whispered as he squeezed Janita's hand and moved to the seat directly behind the railing. The bailiff announced, "All rise, the Honorable A.M. Gaines, presiding."

Attorney Spratt waited patiently while two cases were called ahead of Janita. Jeff began to worry that he would not be through with this case before his ten o'clock scheduled court appearance. When the first two arraignments had been completed, the bailiff finally called the third case.

"Docket number 112143, Janita Alice' Morgan."

"Janita Alice' Morgan, how do you plea."

"Not guilty," Janita nervously replied.

Bail was set at $300,000 and Attorney Spratt announced that they would post bail later. Immediately, following the arraignment Janita was rushed out of the side door to be returned to her cell.

Confused, Junior waited on the steps for Jeff and upon Jeff's arrival, Junior had questions.

"Man, what in the hell's going on? Why did you delay posting bail? You know we can post her bail, right now."

"Calm down, Junior, your sister needs the time to mentally be prepared to face the family. Unfortunately, I agree with that because it'll be very hard on her, Julie and Malcolm. Junior, you have to remember that the victim and the accused are both part of the same family and may I add, a very close family."

"Uncle Jeff, we need to get her out, we can help her."

"I know we can but we need to also help Julie handle the loss of her daughter. Junior, I know you're worried about Janita's safety but she is protected and is alone in her cell."

"How can I tell Pop that Janita doesn't want to come home?"

"You don't have to tell Joseph anything. Janita or I will tell Joe because this is Janita's decision regarding her life and as her attorney I have to do as she requests. Junior, I have a case scheduled for ten o'clock so I really have to go but we'll discuss this later."

"I'm sorry, Uncle Jeff, I shouldn't have questioned Janita's decision, but it hurts to see my sister in handcuffs and I want her home. We all miss her."

Jeff nodded his head in agreement, shook Junior's hand and walked away.

"Oh, Junior, I forgot to tell you that your father will be visiting with Janita between two and three this afternoon. I'm sure everything will be fine so please trust your Uncle Jeff."

CHAPTER
TEN

Following the arraignment, Junior decided to go directly
to Julie's house. Upon his arrival he could see that she had been
crying. As he entered the den, he greeted Julie's husband,
Malcolm. Malcolm mumbled something that could not be
understood by Junior, and Malcolm quickly walked out of the
room. Tears began to roll down Julie's cheeks. Junior walked
over to his sister and put his arms around her. Julie began to sob
uncontrollably. Junior did not know what to do or what to say
so he just held his sister in his arms. As he stood there, Junior
heard the door open. Without saying a word to his wife,
Malcolm walked out the front door. Julie cried out in pain and
Junior led his sister to the sofa and forced her to sit down. He
walked to the bathroom, wet a washcloth with cold water and
returned to the living room where he wiped his sister's face.

"Where are the pills that your doctor prescribed for you
on Saturday?"

"Malcolm threw them out," she sobbed.

"Why," Junior angrily questioned?

"He's crazy. He said he wanted me to feel the same hurt
that he was feeling."

Julie leaned her head on the back of the sofa as she
continued to cry out. Junior walked over to the phone, beeped
Jeanette, walked to the kitchen and poured a glass of water for
his sister. Upon his return, Julie had calmed and was now sitting
quietly on the sofa with her eyes closed. However, her eyes

opened wide as the phone rang. Trying not to disturb Julie, Junior rushed over to answer the phone.

"Hello, Lee's residence."

"Hey, Bro, what's up"?

"Lil Sis, I need for you to contact Julie's doctor for a refill of her prescription .".."

"Junior," Jeanette interrupted, "it's too soon to get a refill. I know she couldn't have taken all of those pills. What happened to them?"

"Jeanette, she did not take all of those pills, your stupid brother-in-law discarded them."

"What," Jeanette shouted. "Is that fool crazy? Julie needed that medicine. That's just like Malcolm, always thinking about himself and throwing money away, especially if it ain't his money. He did not pay for that medicine, I did, and now he has decided to throw it away."

"Jeanette, I don't disagree with you but now is not the time for you to lose it because I really can't handle both of you freaking out at the same time. I need you over here ASAP with that medicine."

"You're right, Junior. I'll see you as soon as I can get a few of my meetings canceled."

Junior wondered if it would be wise for the hotheaded Jeanette to come over to excite Julie's anger. He immediately suggested that she not cancel today's meeting because she might need to be available for Julie tomorrow. Junior recommended to Jeanette that she get the prescription written and that he and Julie would drive over to the hospital and pick it up from her. Jeanette agreed but reminded Junior that she would have to contact the doctor in order to explain why a new prescription was needed. Jeanette asked Junior to beep her upon his arrival to the hospital so that she could walk the medicine out to the car, which would eliminate his need to park.

"Junior, I'm sorry for mouthing off a few minutes ago."

"Jeanette that's okay. You and I both know how you are."

"Junior, go to hell."

Junior chortled and hung up the phone. When Junior turned to look at Julie, she had dosed off to sleep. He picked up the chenille throw and covered her. Julie snuggled and curved her body into a little ball. As she slept, Julie looked peaceful to her brother, but he knew she slept with a broken heart that mourned not only for her deceased daughter, but also for a husband who was not worthy of her love.

Junior walked into the kitchen to keep from disturbing Julie. He sat at the kitchen table, picked up the phone and called his office to check his messages. Two messages were from his associate: the first message asked him about the status of the monthly reports and the second message apologized about his insensitivity during his family's time of mourning. Junior thought, "Perhaps, I need to meet with him to have our duties re-assigned a month earlier than I had planned."

Junior also had a message from his Pop informing him of his afternoon appointment to visit Janita. Junior decided not to return his father's call because he did not want to have him learn about the state of his sister's marriage to that inconsiderate SOB. Junior knew that the Senior Morgan could always sense when something was wrong with the Morgan siblings. He whispered, "Sorry, Pop but I'll call you back later."

Junior sat at the kitchen table remembering how Julie always defended her husband. Malcolm neglected his daughter, had two affairs, had a gambling problem and was always venturing into some half thought-out business deal that in most instances failed. Junior thought, "I've never criticized Malcolm to other members of the family but I cannot nor will I allow him to abuse my sister."

Junior continued to think about his sister's situation and he remembered how smart his mother had been when she prepared her will regarding Julie's inheritance. Junior thought,

"Mother really understood Julie's weakness for allowing Malcolm to spend money on any lamebrain idea that he could find." Jacquelyn's will released only $50,000 directly to Julie, and to no one's surprise Julie allowed Malcolm to take $20,000 of that to invest in his music studio. It was Julie's inheritance that bought that studio but Malcolm always said the studio was his and he did not allow Julie to visit the studio." In deep thought, Junior sat alone in the kitchen, drinking iced tea, when he heard the soft voice of the sweetest Morgan girl.

"A penny for your thoughts," Julie said.

"Honey, I get big bucks for my thoughts, after all I'm about to receive my Ph.D."

Junior smiled, stood up, walked toward Julie.

"How are you feeling? Can I get something for you?"

"Fine and no, but I want to thank you for coming here when you did. That was great timing, Big Brother. Malcolm was so angry with me and for the first time in our marriage I was afraid that he might hit me."

"What," Junior shouted? "He better not ever lay a hand on you, because I will get involved."

"Calm down, Junior. It's not going to be like that because I will leave Malcolm before I allow physical abuse. Unfortunately, I have accepted mental abuse far too long and I promise you, it's going to stop. You know, during one of our many daily arguments, since Amber's death, I commented that our sorrow should be bringing us closer but our marriage is worse than it has ever been. Of course, he blamed our family, especially Janita. I asked Malcolm to wait until after the investigation before he turned his back on Janita but he exploded. I also reminded him that Janita had recently loaned him $5000. I learned about that because I overheard his conversation with his bookie. He told Janita that he needed the money to make an emergency purchase for the studio and that the accountant was out of town. Janita believed him and loaned him the money, but she did not tell me because he convinced her that he didn't want

51

me to worry about the business. When I reminded him of this, he told me that it was none of my damn business and that Janita would probably not even miss that money.

During another argument, I also commented how he had neglected his daughter and even though Amber loved him dearly, she didn't know him. Malcolm was never around nor did he ever do anything with Amber. Junior, Amber did more with you and Pop than she did with her own father and I made the mistake of telling him that today. You know, I think Malcolm's guilt is causing him to lash out at everyone. Malcolm knows that I love him. He knows that most women would have left him long ago. But most of all, he knows that Amber was my heart, my love, my baby. He also knows that Janita is my best friend but it doesn't seem to matter to him that I'm hurting so very much. I need him now to be here for me as I have always been there for him but no, he is selfishly involved in his own personal feelings and I'm being neglected. And now, not only does my heart hurt for Amber and Janita but it also hurts because of him."

Helplessly, Junior listened as Julie lamented, then he realized that he had to get her out of that house.

"Where is your purse?"

Julie pointed. Junior retrieved the purse for her, led her out of the door to his car and he drove off toward the hospital to pick up the medicine from Jeanette.

CHAPTER
ELEVEN

At exactly two o'clock, Paul Mason walked into Jeff Spratt's office.

"Good afternoon, Amy, how are you?"

"Hi, Paul. I'm fine, please have a seat for a few minutes. Jeff is on the phone. He'll be with you shortly."

Paul sat down in the waiting area. He immediately became absorbed in the decorum of the area. His eyes focused on a gigantic aquarium that lined the west wall. Paul recalled Jeff's enthusiasm about an article that he read in a hospital magazine that explained the calming effect the aquarium had on patients and their family members in the hospital setting. Jeff had gotten so involved in the article, he made an appointment with the Morgan lady that worked at St. Theresa's Hospital to discuss the details about the aquarium and to confirm the positive results that were outlined in the article. Following that meeting, Jeff was sold on the idea of aquatic therapy because he was convinced he could better assist his clients if their minds were more relaxed when he met with them. Later, Jeff made a decision to invest a large sum of money into his aquarium and he contracted with a pet store to set up and maintain the aquarium.

Paul glanced at his watch and he realized that Jeff was about fifteen minutes behind schedule. Paul chuckled to himself thinking, obviously that aquatic therapy trickery works because you're not cognizant of the appointment delay when you're

53

engrossed in the inhabitants of the aquarium. Paul's thoughts were interrupted when Jeff walked into the waiting area.

"I'm sorry, Paul but I added to my schedule against Amy's advice and now I am paying for it."

"Thank you for adding me to your schedule."

"Paul, you know that it's important for us to meet whenever you have any information to share with me regarding this case."

"Yes, Jeff, I'm aware of its urgency and I have every available investigator assigned to it."

"Thanks, Paul. By the way, I want to thank you for helping me with my pet therapy project for prisoners. Your two dogs were the first to complete their training and they were the first to make the visits to the correctional facility."

"My mother is committed to this project and she is soliciting other senior citizens who are pet owners. Many of our elders are afraid of the prisoners but Mom tries to convince them they'll be safe because the dogs are not only trained to be therapists for the prisoners but are also trained to protect the owners."

"When Jeanette Morgan shared the hospital's pet therapy program with me, I immediately thought about the hostility and the anger in the prisons that we experience every time we visit a client. If pet therapy could be successful with the ill, why not try it with prisoners who in most cases are mentally ill. While it is too soon to evaluate this new prison program, the warden has asked for additional pets and he has had many prisoners volunteer to assist with the training of the pets. The guards learned that many of the lifers had previously owned pets and are very interested in the program. The pet therapy committee is trying to establish two step-training programs whereby the prisoners will train for the dog therapy visits and the policemen will train the animals to be guard dogs. The committee was concerned and rightfully so, about some smart prisoner training a dog to attack the prison guards; therefore, they decided to partner an inmate dog trainer with a police dog trainer."

Jeff continued, "Man, the prisoners and the guards are all in love with your two Weimeraners, Sonny and Freddo and with your mother's personality, the program is a hit. Well, I guess that's enough about pet therapy for today. So, Paul, what do you have for me today?"

Paul removed a folder from his brief case, and handed it to Jeff.

"My investigation is not complete but I wanted to update you in case you needed the information to discuss with your client."

Jeff placed the report on his desk and this signaled to Paul to continue with the oral report.

"Jeff, Janita has a squeaky clean reputation except for unfounded accusations from a former employee."

"Is it the creep that is discussed in the Morgans' tape or is it the accusation regarding her sexual orientation?"

"I see you have also been doing a little investigating and yes, it is that creep. I met with Olivia Jenkins who was a friend….."

"Yes," Jeff interrupted. "I know Olivia."

"Olivia, a formerly married schoolteacher, left her husband after two years of marriage because her lesbian hair stylist and a lesbian banker had seduced her. Olivia was young, naive and felt very guilty so she decided to leave her wealthy husband. When Mr. Jenkins died, he and Olivia had been separated for thirteen years, however, he left everything to Olivia. There are many rumors about how Olivia acquired her wealth but the truth is, a wealthy man truly loved her. Olivia told me that she and her husband remained friends even after the separation and she knows he had heard the rumors; however, he never once mentioned or questioned her life style. When Olivia met Mrs. Morgan, she had already inherited her money from her husband and by that time she had become celibate. Throughout their friendship, Jacquelyn Morgan did introduce Ms. Jenkins to several eligible men, but none of the men became anything other than friends.

About three years ago, when Mrs. Morgan decided to open the center, she discussed her plans with Olivia. Olivia was extremely grateful that her friend allowed her to plan and operate the center with her. For the first year, Olivia was not paid but she did not mind because she had never made a major donation nor had she volunteered for any worthwhile venture. The years working at the Center were happy except for issues involving the guy or the "creep" that worked at the center."

"What went wrong," Jeff inquired?

"An old friend from Olivia's hometown, somewhere in North Carolina contacted her and asked her to please try to help her son get a job. He had been laid off but would do any type of work in order to pay his rent. Even though other acquaintances from North Carolina warned Olivia not to hire the spoiled troublemaker, she remembered her childhood friendship with this lady, ignored all the advice she had received and hired the young man, Tyrone Battle."

"So, the creep has a name. Tyrone Battle, huh."

"For the first month, Tyrone, who had a teaching degree, was an asset to the center. However, that was short lived. Later, he started to be tardy for work, miss days, and when he did go to work, some of his shady friends started visiting him at the center. By the end of the second month, Olivia decided, with Mrs. Morgan's approval, to fire Tyrone but Mr. Battle had other plans. From some of his hometown folks he had learned about Olivia's past so he decided if Olivia tried to fire him, he would blackmail her by telling Mrs. Morgan and all of their coworkers of her past. Olivia did not fire him on that day. However, she wrote up her meeting with Tyrone as an employee counseling and she told him that if he did not improve within the next two weeks, she would fire him. Tyrone thought that Olivia would be protective of her past life and would be afraid to go through with her plans to terminate him; therefore, he made no attempt to improve. Two weeks later, Olivia had not seen any improvement in Tyrone so she made a decision to fire him. On the day before Mrs. Morgan's death, Olivia met with Jacqueline Morgan to tell her about Tyrone and how he wanted to blackmail her because of her past. Mrs. Morgan got extremely upset about Tyrone but Olivia decided at that time that she needed to share information with her boss, her friend."

Olivia said she would never forget that conversation with Mrs. Morgan because it was the hardest discussion or confession that she had ever made. She remembered saying, "Jackie, before you get upset with Tyrone, please let me tell you about my past."

"Your past is your business. It should not concern Tyrone or me."

Olivia interrupted Mrs. Morgan because she thought it was important for her to know about the lesbian encounters. However, her friend shocked Olivia when she told her that she had known about that since before the two of them had met. Olivia could not believe that the secret that she had protected was never a secret. Jacquelyn reminded Olivia that before the two of them had met, they both had accounts at the same bank, they both had Gigi as their hair stylist at Lynelles Hair Salon, and as in any community, gossip is rampant especially at Lynelles. Jacquelyn explained to Olivia that Mural, the bank vice president, was Jacquelyn's personal banker and Mural let the world know that she was in love with a married woman by the name of Olivia Jenkins. Later when Olivia and Mrs. Morgan met, Mural would always inquire about Olivia Jenkins so it did not take a rocket scientist to figure out that Olivia Jenkins, the new friend was the same Olivia Jenkins, the former lover of Mural, the banker.

Jacquelyn told Olivia to go home for the night and not to worry about Mr. Battle because it was now her responsibility to handle the problem. Jacquelyn had made the decision to fire Tyrone Battle in the morning. However, Mrs. Morgan died the next morning before she could fire him. Janita Morgan became the new director and Tyrone became her nemesis."

"Wow," said Jeff, "No matter how well you think you know someone you never know about the skeletons in that person's closet. Man, I need a drink after that story. Would you like a soda, coffee, juice or water?"

"Water would be fine."

Jeff picked up the receiver of his intercom and asked Amy to please get some water for Paul and a grape soda for him. "Man, are you still hooked on those grape drinks."

"I guess I am. I have really enjoyed that soda throughout the years--are you sure that you don't want one?"

"No, thank you."

Amy tapped on the office door and walked into the office, followed by one of the employees from the bar downstairs in the complex.

"Paul, I ordered the bottle of water but I also ordered you a grape drink just in case you decide to enjoy the delicious soda that my boss enjoys so much."

"No thanks, Amy."

Jeff tasted his drink and said, "Paul, it really is delicious. It makes you feel like a boy again."

"Give me the damn drink," Paul said. He immediately took a swallow of the soda. Amy laughed and as she left the office, Paul whispered, "Not bad, not, bad, thanks, Amy."

"Paul," Jeff said, "are you telling me that Tyrone's job was saved by the death of Jacquelyn Morgan."

"Yes and no. Yes, temporarily, but Janita Morgan is a pistol and very sharp. Without Olivia telling her a word regarding her troubles, Janita was not satisfied with Tyrone's behavior, his attendance, and his socializing on the job. During the first week of management, she was constantly on his back to improve. He was angry and he started asking other employees if they had ever seen Janita with a man. Later he started rumors about Janita having an affair with Olivia. Then one morning,

Janita pulled all of Tyrone's personnel records and she summarized all of the problems that they had been having with him. She called him into her office and she terminated him. She had already alerted security to be outside of her door so after she fired him, she buzzed for them and security escorted Mr. Battle to his car. Olivia said that Janita did not have to give Tyrone a month's pay, but she did authorize the payment to him. After he received his check, Tyrone harassed Janita daily but she did not seem to be afraid or worried about him. Eventually, Tyrone's harassment stopped and the center was better off without Mr. Battle. Janita had won the respect and loyalty of all of her employees." Paul added, "Jeff, Janita is a very popular boss at the center and her employees admire and respect her."

"What does Tyrone Battle do now?"

"Well, that is where my investigation is now but I will tell you this, whatever it is, it is illegal. I am sure that I will have additional details for you later today. Jeff, I'm sure that I do not have to ask you to please be careful with the information regarding Olivia. Even though Olivia doesn't mind her personal information released, especially if it will help Janita, I think we need to be careful and not disrupt her life. Olivia is really a very nice lady, and she has dedicated her life to the center. I wish that she could find someone nice to share her life."

"Paul, I do know Olivia and I will not divulge any details unless it is absolutely necessary. However, my gut tells me that Janita will be against any of this information being discussed in court. Your report does, however, give us a motive for Tyrone to frame Janita and it also give me a clue regarding the prosecutor's case." Jeff continued, "Paul, I would like everything that you can find on Mr. Tyrone Battle and I would like it PDQ. Somehow, that creep is involved in this case. I know it, you know it and the Morgan family knows it, so let's prove it. Paul, please call me on my cell phone as soon as you have details about Tyrone. It doesn't matter the time, day or night. Keep in touch."

"Will do," Paul said, and he left Jeff's office.

CHAPTER
TWELVE

Joseph Morgan nervously sat in the visitor's area of the jail, awaiting the arrival of his daughter, Janita. He was thankful that his friend, the Chief had allowed him to visit with Janita before the arraignment. Joseph sat and outlined all the things that he had to do for his daughter:

I must be strong for her.
I must let her talk.
I must listen to her.
I must do whatever she requests.

Joseph remembered that Janita sounded much better when she left the message on the answering machine. He thought, I don't want her to become withdrawn again because we need her to remember what happened so that we can fight to get her out of this horrible place.

Janita walked up without being noticed by her father.

"Hi, Pop, how are you?"

Joseph jumped up, smiled and stared at his daughter.

"Baby, I'm fine but the question is, how are you doing?"

"Considering where I am, I am doing okay but I'm fortunate to have protectors who work here that watch over me."

"Honey, do you have any idea when they have scheduled your hearing so that we can get you out of this place?"

"Pop, it was this morning. Now, don't be angry because I ordered my lawyer, your friend, Uncle Jeff not to tell you because I was not ready to face my family. I'm still not able to answer any questions regarding that night and with not knowing what happened that night, I could never face Julie and Malcolm."

"Baby, I should have been there this morning."

"Pop, I knew that you wanted to be there but I did not want you to see me with handcuffs and leg shackles. Look at me, Pop. I feel like an animal with these handcuffs around my wrists."

"Did Jeff say how long it will it take to have bail posted?"

"I'm sorry and I hope you'll try to understand this but I also asked Uncle Jeff to delay posting bail."

"What!" "Why did you do that?"

"Pop, wait, listen to me first before you get too upset. I need to be stronger before I can face Julie and Malcolm. Julie allowed me to take care of her daughter, Friday night, and Pop, I failed to do that. Now, my Godchild is dead and I can't even remember what happened. I need time and no matter what Julie tells you, she needs time. How is she doing, Pop?"

"Julie is still grieving and I really have not seen Malcolm since the funeral. Julie is very concerned about you, and she really does miss you."

"Has Malcolm been there for Julie?"

"I would think so," Joseph replied, "or is something going on that you two have not shared with me?"

"Pop, I asked the question because I am concerned about what is happening with them as they mourn for Amber. I know the pain and it's almost unbearable."

"Honey, I understand but I'm your parent and when you're in pain, I am also in pain. I'm sorry for pressuring you but I need to get you out of here."

"Okay, Pop. Can we change the subject because we only have a few minutes for this visit."

"Alright baby. Honey, can you remember anything about that night?"

"I have tried to remember the details but I can't remember anything. I have been thinking about asking Uncle Jeff to request

61

permission to consult with a psychiatrist because I've never lost my memory in the past."

Joseph listened intently to his daughter, then he said, "Janita, when you return to your cell perhaps you could sit down, relax, close your eyes, and try to remember one thing about that night. Then, slowly move your thoughts, methodically, forward or backwards and you may be able to recall more about the evening."

"That might help. I'll try that this afternoon."

"Oh, by the way honey, I met with Olivia on Tuesday and I asked her to manage the center until your return. She agreed and later she called me about signing a check for supplies that would be arriving on Wednesday. Baby, the center really looks great. Your mother would be very proud of you for keeping her dream alive, functioning and running well. I'm so proud of you, my dear."

"Thanks, Pop," Janita said with tears swelling in her eyes but before she could say anything else she was interrupted with an announcement.

"May I have your attention please. May I have your attention please. Five minutes remaining for visiting hours. Five minutes remaining for visiting hours."

"Baby, I want you home with me. I want you out of this place."

"Pop, I know that you want me home, and I will come home." Then she noticed Franklin approaching and she decided to introduce her father to George, her former high school classmate.

"Mr. Morgan, I believe that your daughter is innocent and if there is anything that I can do for you, please let me know. Sir, I think that you should know that when Janita is released, I'm hoping that she'll allow me to see her socially."

Janita was shocked and a little embarrassed at Franklin's comments and was equally as surprised at her father's response.

"Thank you, Son, and perhaps my daughter will invite you to my house for a visit."

The two men shook hands and Franklin walked off.

"Mr. George Franklin seems like a nice young man who seems interested in my daughter, so now I guess I'll just have to wait and see if my daughter is interested in the young man."

"Oh, Daddy, please don't tease me. George is just a former classmate."

"Okay, baby. If you believe that, then I believe it."

Janita looked at her father and smiled.

"It is certainly nice to see such a beautiful smile on your face as I leave today. Perhaps, I should thank Mr. Franklin who is just a former classmate. Good-bye darling."

"Good-bye Daddy. Please tell everyone that I love them, I miss them and that I'll be home very soon."

CHAPTER THIRTEEN

Chief Ronald Petit called the lab to inquire about the results of the fingerprints that had been dusted off of the glasses located in the Morgan house.   The clerk asked the Chief to hold on for the director.

"Hi Ron, this is Dottie Robito. We do have a match for two glasses, the victim and the accused but the third glass was spotless. However, it was obvious that it had been wiped clean."

"Umm. Robito, something seems rotten in Denmark, wouldn't you say?"

"Yes, I agree.   Ron, we checked that entire living room for prints.   We didn't find prints any place except those two glasses that were used by the victim and the accused. That room was wiped clean by professionals."

"Um, why would professionals be involved in this case? Dottie, what about outside the door? Did you find any prints?"

"I found one strange print on the outside near the door but I would like to caution you that we still have not placed that print inside the house."

"Are you saying that there was only *one* print on the entire outside door?"

"Yes, that is exactly what I am saying. There were no prints on the doorbell or the door. It was wiped clean. However, they may have left something for you to use with your investigation.   The guest that entered Janita Morgan's home pressed the door bell with *his* left index finger."

"So, Dottie, you believe that we have a male southpaw, huh."

"Yes. Our visitor was a male. A lefty. Ron, picture this."

"This sounds freaky. Go on, Dottie, I'm listening."

"When he placed his left index finger on the doorbell his left thumb rested on the door casing as he rang the doorbell. Not realizing this, he failed to wipe the thumb print from the door casing."

"Son-of-a-gun," Ron shouted, "and could you find a match for that print."

"Yes, the print belongs to a Tyrone Battle, who seems to be a small time bookie, however, he has very little on his record."

"Thanks, Dottie. Great job."

"I will fax the written report right now to the number that's recorded on the accession card. Take care, Ron and good luck with your case."

Ronnie hung up the phone, completed his notes and shouted to Franklin to check the fax machine for a confidential report that should be arriving very shortly. As he organized his note, Franklin walked in and Ronnie asked him to close the door and to have a seat. Franklin handed the report to the Chief and he pulled out his note pad to receive his assignment.

"Franklin, find out everything that you can on Tyrone Battle who may be a two bit bookie. See if you can connect him to Janita Morgan or anyone in the Morgan family. I would prefer that you not ask Janita about him or mention his name to her."

"No sir, I would never do that. Sir, should I assume that this is priority?"

"Yes, do whatever you can to start your investigation today and if you need to leave the office, do so, because I will be in the office this afternoon. By the way, when does Chris Gude return from his vacation?"

"Sir, he'll be returning on Monday, and I would like to thank you for allowing me to act as your assistant during Lieutenant Gude's vacation. I have gained so much from this experience. Chief, I'll be leaving shortly after I complete a computer search on Mr. Battle. However, I'm waiting for a call from the DA for information on the Cunningham case. In my absence, I'll have the desk clerk forward the call to you. Sir, I'll bring the folder in before I leave."

"Good luck, Franklin. You have done well with the men this week."

Franklin left the office and immediately went to his computer to begin retrieving information on Mr. Battle. When Ronnie saw him at the computer, he thought, 'those young guys retrieve so much from that damn thing. One day, I hope to learn how to maneuver through those programs with ease.' Ronnie returned his thoughts to the Morgan case and he considered contacting Jeff, Janita's attorney to discuss the case but he decided to wait for Jeff to contact him. He sat down and decided to read in detail the report that was faxed to him by Dottie Robito, the lab director.

CHAPTER
FOURTEEN

In an attempt to remember what had happened that night, Janita Morgan decided to try what her father had recommended. She laid back on her cot, closed her eyes and relaxed but instead of that night, her mind shifted to George Franklin's comment to her father. She thought, 'he is better looking than he was in high school and he is such a gentleman. I guess the military improved on what was already there.' Her mind returned to her present situation and she whispered, "Boy, I've always had bad luck with men. He's the first man that I've been interested in for some time and now it happens when I'm in this place. I may not ever get a chance to see him as anything other than an officer." Janita realized that she was feeling sorry for herself, and beginning to think, "poor, pitiful, Janita." Tears began to swell her eyes and as she fought to hold back the tears, Janita vowed to do whatever necessary to get out of that horrible place.

Janita closed her eyes and for the first time since her incarceration she saw Amber, her godchild, her niece, her heart and Janita began to cry. She could even see this beautiful little girl in the coffin and her entire body began to hurt. She cried out in pain and one of the officers asked her if she needed something, or if she was ill.

"No, I don't need help." Janita cried, "I miss my godchild so much." Janita continued to cry out in pain.

The lady in the cell next to Janita became concerned and tried to comfort her.

"Baby, let it out," she whispered. "You need to cry. I know it's hard for a girl like you to be locked up like an animal but if you're innocent someone will solve your case."

"I did not hurt her. I could never hurt her. I love her too much. I want to go home."

As Janita cried, the lady continued to softly whisper in a soothing tone until Janita could cry no more. With her eyes closed, Janita lay on the cot in deep thought for about fifteen minutes. Slowly, she began to remember the afternoon that she had visited with Amber. Janita remembered the dinner that she and her sister, Julie, had prepared while Amber packed her clothes to spend the night. Janita smiled about the number of clothes that Amber had packed. She thought about their drive from Julie's home to her house. Amber had convinced Janita to stop at the mall to buy writing tablets with all kinds of fancy pencils.

Janita had always thought that Amber was gifted. She had asked Julie on several occasions to have Amber tested but Julie always claimed she did not know where to have her tested. By the time that Amber was two years old, she could print her name, and she could also identify letters when viewed backwards through windows or through mirrors. At three years of age, Amber could print her mother's and father's names and could spell many other words. Amber loved to write and by the time she was six years old, everyone had to watch what was said in Amber's presence because she had a talent to write everything down that she heard. At first, the family considered Amber's talent for writing as *cute* but later it became an aggravation, because it was difficult to talk in front of her. Everyone in the family was aware of Amber's talent and everyone believed that oneday she would write a bestseller book. But now, that could never happen. Amber was gone. Amber would never be back. She would never write that bestseller. Janita raised her aching body from her cot and quietly sat on the side. Janita longed to see Amber. She wanted to hold her again. Slowly, her thoughts

68

drifted to that day; the day that took her niece and shattered her world.

When Janita and Amber left the mall, Amber had convinced her Aunt Janita to buy notebooks, popcorn, apple juice, hair ribbon, pencils and a gift for her Mommy.

The next stop for the happy duo was Verdelle's Ice Cream Shop for the dessert that they had not had with their dinner. Amber was thrilled with this surprise. Janita recalled how much fun she and Amber had inside of the ice cream shop. Amber had talked constantly and the two of them had laughed at everything. Janita wondered if Amber would grow up to be a comedy writer because she was very comical. As Janita sat across from Amber, for the first time she realized how much Amber resembled her grandmother, Jacquelyn Morgan. Amber had a gorgeous face with keen features and thick, long, dark brown hair that was twisted in thick locks. Janita remembered thinking that Amber could be a model and she wondered if she should give her modeling classes for her birthday. However, that thought faded fast because the picture of Fon Renee, the adult looking baby model, flashed in her mind. Janita decided that it would be better to allow Amber to remain a little girl a while longer and continue her dancing and gymnastic classes.

Janita remembered thinking how blessed Julie and Malcolm were to have had such a beautiful and talented daughter. Janita recalled how Amber had stood in the aisle of the ice cream shop to show her Nanny the new dance that her Mommy taught her. Amber was a great dancer and as Janita and all the other customers at Verdelles watched Amber do her dance in the aisle, Janita overheard one of the customers comment, "That child is a great dancer." Janita could see that Amber had inherited her parent's talent for dancing. She remembered how well Julie and Malcolm danced together. Janita would often tease Julie by telling her that dancing was the only thing that she and her husband had in common.

Finally, after two hours since their departure from Julie's house, Janita and Amber arrived at Janita's house. Amber decided to unpack and place all of her clothes in the dresser drawers. Then she returned to the living room with a video movie to watch and she asked for popcorn. Janita told her she was a pig and since she had just had ice cream it was too soon to eat popcorn. Janita smiled as she recalled how Amber laughed when she was called a pig and she skipped around the room saying, "Oink, oink, oink. I'm a pig. Oink, oink, oink, I'm a pig." Janita remembered that the phone rang and that she quieted Amber as she answered the phone but she could not remember who had called her. She struggled in her mind trying to identify the caller but suddenly she was roused with an announcement by the guard who shouted, "Dinner."

CHAPTER
FIFTEEN

Jeff Spratt's secretary, Amy tapped on the door, walked into Jeff's office and for the first time since she worked for him she found him leaning back in his chair with feet propped on top of his desk. Amy knew that the Morgan case was weighing heavily on his mind but in the past Jeff had never placed his feet on his beautiful, expensive desk. She walked into Jeff's office, sat on the chair in front of him and waited for him to say something. Anything. He did not.

"Do you need to talk?" Amy asked.

"You know, Joseph Morgan is closer to me than my own damn, jealous biological brother. The two of us have been there for each other through all types of problems but with this murder, I am not sure how much more my friend can handle."

"Jeff, I can't believe this. You can't get depressed about this case. At this time, you should be trying to lift Mr. Morgan spirits and make him feel better. You need to visit him and find something other than the case to talk about or maybe you can take him out to dinner or go get a drink. Boss, you know your friend is a strong and proud man but the most important function that he has had to perform is being a father. No matter what happens with this case, he'll be strong in order to hold his family together, and, as you have done in the past, you'll be there with him."

Not hearing the door open, Amy and Jeff were both startled when Joseph Morgan interrupted Amy.

"Jeff, she is correct except for one thing, we do know what will happen with this case. Janita is innocent and she will be home soon."

"Good evening, sir, I'll leave you friends alone."

"Thanks, Amy," Jeff said. "Why don't you call it a day?"

"Your calendar is in your folder with all of the papers that you will need for tomorrow. Good-bye, Jeff, I'll see you in the morning. Good-night, Mr. Morgan."

"Good-night, Amy."

Jeff stood and walked over to Joseph. The two friends shook hands.

"How are you doing, pal?"

"Perhaps better than you're doing. Jeff, I do appreciate your concern for my family and me but I can't have my best bud wimp on me. Man, I need you to help me find out who killed my granddaughter. I want my Janita home and cleared of this crime."

"You're right, Joe. We'll get her out of this mess and we'll clear her name. Now, Buddy, how are you doing? I was about to have a grape soda, would you like one?"

"No, but I would like one of those beers that you have stashed away."

Jeff smiled and said, "That does sound better than the grape soda, and since I'm officially closed, I'll also have a beer."

As Jeff got the beer from his personal hidden refrigerator that was built into his desk, the two friends were quiet and seemed to be in deep thought. Jeff sat on the chair across from Joseph and they both sipped from their beer.

"For the center to be such a good thing for the community, it seems to me that every time there is a flicker of success, a death occurs in my family."

"I realize the center is a memorial to Jacquelyn but if it causes so much pain, perhaps you should consider closing it."

"Our family has never considered it a memorial to Jacquelyn. It's a business that supports my daughter and others on her staff. The center was opened and is opened because Jacquelyn believed that there was a need for a hideaway for the children between eight and twelve years old, the 'tweenies' as she so lovingly called them. Jackie believed that age group considered themselves too old for a day care center while most of the parents believed that their eight to ten year olds were too young to be left alone. The project targeted the latch key kids and the center started with a very small number of children. Today there are 139 students enrolled in the program."

Jeff noticed how Joe's attitude improved and his desolate expression brightened as he discussed the Tween Center. Jeff immediately remembered Amy's advice and he decided to pursue the discussion regarding the center.

"What's the purpose of the center or how does the program work?"

"In order to be registered, the child must be enrolled into a school and pay a registration fee. There's also a weekly fee that must be paid in advance."

"The center seems similar to the afterschool care program, so why would a parent enroll their child at the center?"

"Good question, my friend. They come because of what the center has to offer the students. When the students arrive at the center, they must first go to the Cave to complete or start their homework. Janita has tutors from the university to assist the students with their school assignments. In the cave or library as I call it, free snacks are provided and the staff plays that noisy rap music. According to Janita that is the way the children of today do their homework."

"Do you know what type of grades those students are making in their classes?"

"Of course. All are now A and B students but prior to their enrollment at the Tween Center, sixty-five percent were below a "C" level.

"As I recall, Janita's degree is in education. Isn't it?"

"Yes, her undergraduate degree is in education but she also has an MBA. Janita is really great with her staff and they seem to be one happy family. Even the students seem happy over there. After the students complete their homework, they can go to any of the other areas to participate in projects that interest them. In the game room, there are pool tables and pinball machines. Refreshments are sold in the game room. They often have live entertainment from that rapper they call PeeDoubleE. Janita thinks that he communicates well with the students and he is also a good influence on the kids, especially the boys. This young man works with Janita to prepare rap songs for a particularly difficult subject or achievement test. I believe Janita selects the material to be covered, the rapper writes the lyrics and Franco performs the music. There is always action in the game room."

"How did Janita meet the rapper?"

"Janita and Franco received their Masters Degrees together and they have remained friends through the years."

"There are two other classrooms at the center. One of them is called the 'Run Way'. TraceAnne, a very attractive lady, teaches grooming, manners, make-up application and God knows what else they do in that room. TraceAnne encourages boys to attend so twice per month she has closed sessions for boys only. Janita had us all laughing because the first male session had only one boy in the class and her staff all wondered if he was gay. However, they are indebted to him because he broke the ice and now the young men have to pre-register to reserve a seat for the male sessions. By the way, the first young man who attended the sessions turned out to be a quarterback at the Rosewood Playground and is very popular with the ladies.

"The other room is called 'Time Out' and Olivia has used that room to counsel and listen to the students with problems. Originally, the sessions were scheduled one hour per day, two days per week. However, because of the demand Olivia now has daily sessions. Janita has also solicited the assistance of the deacon from our church to have prayer service and to my surprise the kids really do attend the prayer services. Jeff, The Tween Center is a very nice, well-run project that is great for the community."

74

"Joe, I'm really embarrassed for not having been to the center and for not knowing anything about it, but I promise you that I'll have Janita give me a tour as soon as she gets back to work. By the way, several times I have driven past the center and I have seen middle age adults either entering or leaving the center. What are they doing at the center?"

"Oh, yes," Joseph laughed, "They are the adult tweens. As you know, the center was an afterschool venture. Therefore, it was really a part-time business. In Janita's quest to extend services she and Olivia initiated and are now piloting a new program for the early retirees who are between the ages of fifty-five and sixty-five. Janita believes early retirees are the forgotten customers who are sandwiched between workers with benefits and Medicare recipients with programs that teach them to stay healthy. The early retirees became the new target that The Tween Center wanted to reach and they have developed programs that may be of interest to the senior tweens."

Joseph paused for a bathroom break. Jeff retrieved two new beers. The conversation continued as soon as Joseph returned to the office,

"Joe, what type of programs did your dynamic duo at the Tween Center decide to provide for the senior tweens?"

Joseph laughed as he accepted the beer from his friend and he teased, "Oh, Mr. Spratt, are you now interested in the center?"

"I really like what I've heard today and I'm becoming very interested in what's going on over there, especially since I can see how elated you become when you discuss the center. Now, Joe, tell me about those old folks."

Joseph laughed as he continued, "The tween seniors pay the same fees as the students and the center offers many programs for them. One morning I watched the class members jump around exercising to that *Seniors Working up a Sweat* video by that little Tamara Lorouzan and that was not a pretty sight."

Jeff joined Joseph in laughing at the vision he imagined of the exercise class. Then Joseph continued his discussion.

"Janita has also networked with the local Retirement Association and they offer the driver refresher course that helps keep insurance costs down. They also have other programs such as investments, baby-sitting with grandchildren, proper shoes to wear, line dancing, traveling, proper use of medication and all kinds of arts and craft junk. Janita and her staff were shocked at the response and she already has a waiting list." Joseph continued, "Man, I went over to the center about three weeks ago, and I was shocked to see those old geezers trying to play those machines in the game room."

Jeff began to laugh as he pictured the old geezer that he had seen in front of the center trying to shoot pool or to play on the pinball machines in the game room.

"Wait, Jeff, man, don't laugh because some of them played very well."

Jeff continued to laugh and Joe joined in the laughter.

"Joe, I'm hungry, would you like to go out to eat?"

"Sounds good to me."

Jeff began to gather his briefs and calendar to leave the office and Joseph discarded the empty bottles. Jeff thought about the 'old' Tweenies and began to laugh again.

"Buddy, leave that trash and let's get out of here. You know, when I go to the center for a tour, I think I'll go in the morning when the adult tweens are there so that I can have another good laugh."

"Thanks Buddy," Joseph whispered. "I know what you've been doing and I do appreciate you taking time from your busy schedule for me. It's helped me tremendously to relax with a friend."

Walking toward the door, Joseph added, "By the way, Jeff, those old geezers that we're laughing at, they're very close to our age." Both friends continued to laugh as they walked out of the office.

76

CHAPTER
SIXTEEN

"Well, well, well, look who we have here," said the young man who was standing outside in front of the Juke Joint Bar as the casually dressed George Franklin, Jr. got out of his car.

"GJ, where have you been?"

Franklin shook Dexter Walters' hand.

"Man, how are you? Don't you remember that I joined the Air Force shortly after graduation?"

"Well, Bro, the hood is still the same; some dudes have jobs, others still stand on the corner, some are in jail, others are about to go to jail, and there are a few like you that either graduated from college or went into the military."

"Are you married? Do you have children?"

Dexter laughed and said, "Yes and no. About nine months ago I was kicked out by my lady and the divorce will be final in a few days. Ain't got no children because that woman would not stay home long enough to take care of a baby. I worked and she played."

"Where do you work?"

"I'm still at the glass factory. Many times, I thought about leaving that place, but because I've been there so long, my salary and my benefits are really great. I guess I'll be there until I retire, die or they lay me off. Come on in, and have a drink with an old high school buddy."

"Sure, why not, but Dexter, you know that I'm not a big drinker."

As Dexter led George into the Juke Joint Bar, he laughed at George's comment.

"Yeah, yeah, I remember, GJ, my boy, you could never really hang when drinking was involved."

When the two men entered the bar, Franklin was reminded of an old television show, because many of the regulars at the bar looked up and greeted them by shouting, "DEEEEEXTERRRRR," just as the TV characters shouted Norm when the fat guy entered his office, the bar. Franklin recognized one or two of the customers but everyone seemed to know Dexter. Franklin and Dexter sat down at one of the small tables and both ordered a beer. As they talked about their parents, siblings and former friends, many of the patrons stopped by the table to speak with Dexter.

"Dexter, I see nothing has changed. You're still very popular with everyone."

"Man, I've been hanging out here in the hood for a very long time; so, yes, a bunch of folks know me. I'm also the part time bartender and you know everyone tells the old bartender every freaking thing."

"Does old man Gray still own this bar?"

"Mr. Gray put the Juke Joint up for sale about five years ago and I purchased it. GJ, I don't tell the people out here that I own this Joint because my relationship with some would probably change and the others would be hitting me for a buck or two. As it is now, most of the customers believe that I'm as broke as they are and that I work here part time as a bartender to make ends meet."

As the two friends talked, one of the patrons went over to the music box and played the old hit, *Chasing the One I love* by Tallie Lance. Old memories immediately surfaced and the two friends laughed and reminisced about what was happening in high school when that song was a hit.

Dexter said, "Man, when that song came out, I was busy chasing Janita Morgan."

"Did you ever catch her?"

Dexter's facial expression changed as he said, "Yes, I did but it didn't last too long because she was one of those good little girls and you know what I wanted."

Dexter's voice tone changed and Franklin hoped that he would discuss Janita Morgan's case.

"Man, I hate what's going down with Janita."

"I do too but for some reason, I can't believe that the girl we went to school with could kill anyone."

"Neither me and in fact I know she didn't do it."

"How do you know it? How can you be so sure that she did not kill her niece?"

"Man, since the murder, that's all everybody talks about Backatown. Of course, that damn Tyrone knows everything about the killing."

"Do I know Tyrone?"

"No, Bro, the dude came around here after you left the hood. Tyrone use to work with Janita at that Tween Center she took over after her mother died but Janita only took a minute of Tyrone's mess. She realized from the get go that the brother ain't no damn good and she got rid of his sorry ass. Now, the dude spends his time hustling brothers, trying to be a little bookie. GJ, you know what, no matter what kind of troubles I may have had in my life, I can honestly say that I ain't ever done illegal shit and I've never taken advantage of anyone. I just don't like misusing people."

"I hear you, bro. Is Tyrone in here right now?"

"No, but just as soon as the lottery numbers are announced on TV at eight fifty seven, Tyrone is going to come out to collect his money."

"If Tyrone is a bookie, why did Janita let him hang around the center?"

"Oh, no," said the smooth talking, slow talking Dexter Walters. "She did not keep him on at the center that long after she became the manager. He tried to give Janita a little trouble about him being fired but Tyrone was banned from the center by that dead girl's daddy."

"Man, you've lost me. What dead girl are you now talking about?"

"George, I'm talking about the little girl that Janita is in jail for killing."

"Is Tyrone close to the Morgan family or to the dead girl's daddy?"

"Hell no. Tyrone is Malcolm's bookie and they meet here for betting transactions. Man, they've been meeting here so often that I've considered charging Tyrone rent for using the Juke Joint as his office. Now, George, just because Malcolm is married to one of the Morgan girls, he ain't a saint."

"Is Malcolm from the hood and if so, do I know him?"

"You don't know him, in fact, I don't really know him. I met him when he started coming in looking for Tyrone to pay his gambling debts."

Franklin's investigative heart begin to pound faster and he realized that he needed to calm down because he did not want to have Dexter think that he was greatly interested in the case.

"Are you saying that one of the Morgans have a gambling problem?"

"Man, Malcolm ain't a Morgan. He is a want-a-be that is living uptown dabbling in small unsuccessful businesses and losing all of his wife's money. He now has a recording studio and he could really be making money with it, but every group that uses the studio complains about how Malcolm tries to take advantage of them. George, a man with a gambling problem or any other kind of addiction can't run a successful business. The addiction will cause any potential or any successful business to fail, every time. I mean every time."

"One of the brothers that gambles with Tyrone claimed that a few months back, Malcolm owed Tyrone money and Janita loaned Malcolm the money. People back here know Tyrone. They know of Malcolm and they are saying Janita didn't kill Malcolm's little girl. And man, you and I both know that Janita ain't gay. With her looks, she could get any man or woman that she wanted so why would she mess around with her little niece and then kill the little girl to keep her quiet."

80

George Franklin was about to suffocate with the important but unbelievable news that he had just heard, so he stood up and began to stutter.

"Man, er, er, do you want another beer?"

"Sure, GJ, but sit down."

Dexter looked over to the bar, raised two fingers, motioned to the empty bottles on the table to indicate exactly what he wanted and the beers were immediately brought over to the table. George decided to ask Dexter about his last statement regarding Janita instead of waiting and hoping that he would continue.

"Dexter, are you telling me that the little girl was molested because I have not heard that before. Was it in the paper?"

"I don't know if it was in the paper, but my man over there behind the bar said that Tyrone told him that Janita had messed with the girl so I assumed that Malcolm had told Tyrone. Now that I'm thinking about it, maybe Malcolm didn't tell Tyrone because I haven't seen Malcolm out here since the girl died. Damn, man, I just hate to see anybody hurt a kid, an innocent little girl."

Dexter and George both sat quietly for a few minutes and both were in deep thought about the comments that had just been made.

"How your mamma and daddy doing?"

"They are both doing well," George replied. You do know that they still live Backatown and in our same house. However, I must admit I do worry about them. You know my parents are still raising babies. At a time in their lives when they could really be enjoying each other, they are busy raising my sister Denise's little girl."

"Where's Denise these days?"

"You do remember that Denise's husband was killed drag racing that damn Mercedes. Man, I believe that my brother-in-law loved that car more than he loved my sister. After his death,

Denise decided that she needed to refocus her life and she joined the air force. She also convinced Mom and Dad to take care of her daughter, Mercedes who of course was named by Denise's husband for his beloved car. She is a cute little girl who has had to grow up very fast. However, she seems to have adjusted very well."

"How are your parents adjusting to Mercedes?"

"You know, quite well. Mom and Dad even act younger and they do things with Mercedes that they didn't have time to do with us. Denise sends Mom a check every month and Mercedes also receives a social security check from her father's death. My parents now have what they call 'extra' retirement money."

"I hate to see old people being taken advantage of by their children but in your sister's case, it seems like it's been good for your parents. I just hope that it's not too hard on little Miss Mercedes being away from her mama like that. George, I do stop by sometimes to check on your parents because I have always liked them and I especially admired how they raised their children. Man, all of you are doing okay."

"Thank you man, I agree. I also think that my parents did their job well. Dexter, I have really enjoyed seeing you again and it has been like old times but I want to go over and see my folks and I need to get there soon because they do go to bed very early."

"Look, man, let's stay in touch."

The two friends shook hands and George walked out the door. Dexter sat down at the table and was in deep thought when suddenly someone sat down next to him and placed an arm around his neck. Dexter looked up.

"George, what's wrong?"

"Man, I have to tell you something," George whispered.

"No, you don't have to tell me anything. Remember what you said earlier, that I seem to know everything that is going on in the hood. George, people talk in the hood, and your occupation has been discussed but I don't like people hurting others and that little Tyrone is hurting too many of our people. Two weeks ago, two Uptown men who work for Tyrone's boss beat up one of the kids that grew up down the street from me. The child owed Tyrone $200 for a gambling debt. George, you know that ain't right. The Negro just ain't no damn good and we need to get him out of the hood and off the streets. Now, do your job but there's one thing that you should remember, I don't routinely talk to cops. Tonight, I talked with an old friend who can use whatever I've said that can free an old classmate and convict those other folks."

"Man, the hood needs more men like you."

Dexter chuckled and said, "George, there are plenty of dudes out here trying to do good just like me. Now, get out of here because if you walk out of the door right now, you can see Tyrone Battle who just drove up in that old white 1965 mustang that he ripped off from one of his 'clients.' Now, go"

As George walked out admiring his friend, he remembered why he was part of Dexter's high school posse. Dexter was the type of person that all of the guys in school wanted to be; an average student, a great athlete, a great dancer, good looks, muscle man, neat dresser, good manners that got him everywhere with the teachers and parents and made him very popular with the girls. Suddenly George's thoughts were interrupted when he heard a grumpy, nasty sounding voice.

"Deven. Deven. You got my goddamn money."

Officer Franklin looked up and immediately made mental notes about a character that he wanted out of the hood, off the streets and in jail.

CHAPTER
SEVENTEEN

Paul Mason reviewed his notes, picked up the phone and dialed Jeff Spratt's cell phone number. Within two rings, the phone was answered.

"Jeff Spratt."

"Sorry to call you so early but do you have time for breakfast?"

"I can make time. When and where?"

"You name it."

Jeff looked at his watch and his appointments for the day.

"Half hour at the Esquire Cafe."

"Great, see you there."

Paul immediately left because he wanted to secure a table in an area where confidential information could be exchanged. Upon his arrival to the cafe, Paul made note of the table arrangements and he realized why Jeff had selected this restaurant. Each table was privately glassed in and there were customers who seemed to be lawyers with their clients being served. Each glassed booth had electrical outlets and a small worktable for laptop computers. Paul was impressed. Jeff arrived shortly after Paul and the maitre d' recognized Attorney Spratt and escorted the two men to what Paul considered Jeff's special table. As soon as Paul and Jeff were seated, the waitress brought in grapefruit juice for Jeff. She had four other glasses of juice for Paul to make a selection. Paul selected the orange juice and as the waitress set the juice in front of Paul, she asked if there were any special needs. Jeff shook his head no, and thanked her. The waitress closed the door behind her.

"Before we start, why not make your selection so that we can order before we begin our discussion."

When both men had decided what to order, Jeff pressed an intercom button and gave his order, then Jeff pointed to Paul's intercom button and Paul gave his order. When Paul had given his order, Jeff pressed the button to indicate the order had been completed and keyed in his PIN number that would transfer his payment for breakfast plus fifteen percent gratuity from his checking account to the Cafe's account.

"Nice," Paul said. "Is this place just for lawyers?"

"No. If that was the case, you know that people in my profession would be the first to sue. Lawyers get rich when businesses try to prevent others from utilizing a facility."

Jeff paused for a minute, sipped a little of his grapefruit juice, and looked at Paul to begin his report.

"What do we have now?"

"Jeff, I am convinced that Mr. Battle either committed the murder or he had someone else do it for him."

"Oh, is he that powerful, to have people kill for him?"

"Powerful, no. Stupid, yes. Mr. Battle is a bookie and works for some of the town's big guns that know how to keep their fingers clean by using their little hustling street bookies. However, Tyrone does have clients all over this great city. He has a college degree and communicates well with many of the city's professionals with gambling problems."

Jeff looked up with inquiring eyes wondering what was Paul about to say next. The conversation was interrupted when the waitress walked in and began to place the ordered food in front of the two customers.

"How did she know who had ordered what?"

Jeff smiled and said, "That's what everyone who eats here for the first time asks. When you pressed your intercom button, it registered your seat location."

"This is really a nice setup," Paul said as he added sugar to his coffee.

Paul's last statement had Jeff's wondering mind roaming wildly and he looked at Paul trying to encourage him to continue his report.

"Paul, you're not saying that the professionals with gambling problems are connected to this case."

"Oh, no, but I can't say that about the little bookie, Mr. Battle. Jeff, Tyrone is not a nice person and he doesn't care who gets hurt in order for him to get his money."

Between discussing the case, and trying to eat, Paul commented to Jeff about the restaurant.

"It's not often that you find a restaurant with a great atmosphere and also great food. I like this place and I am glad you introduced it to me this morning. In the future, I'll have to remember to invite some of my other clients to eat here, especially if they are picking up the tab."

Jeff and Paul both chuckled but the discussion immediately returned to the Morgan case.

"Jeff, I'm not sure where my investigation will lead us but I do have some concerns that I'll share with you."

Jeff looked worried as Paul continued,

"Janita's brother-in-law, Malcolm Lee has a very expensive gambling habit and often owes Tyrone Battle and his bosses a great deal of money."

"Oh, my Lord," Jeff whispered, "please don't tell me that those animals killed that precious little girl because of the gambling debts of the father?"

"Jeff, wait, slow down. I can't prove anything, yet, but we are still searching. I am convinced, however, that there is a connection and I believe that Tyrone Battle was the person that knocked on Janita Morgan's door the night of the murder when Janita was on the phone talking with Jeanette. I also believe that Tyrone was trailing Janita when she had Malcolm's little girl with her and that he was the creep that Janita saw at Clo's Hamburger Shop that afternoon. My sources tell me that Janita had loaned Malcolm $5000 recently supposedly for supplies at his studio,

86

but he actually gave the cash to Tyrone for money that he had gambled and lost."

"Damn," Jeff said, "what in the hell is Malcolm betting on to lose that kind of money?"

"You name it, he bets on it. However, he loses most of his money by betting on the horses. That seems to be his favorite but he also bets on whatever sport is in for that season. I'm afraid that the your friend's son-in-law has a gambling addiction."

Paul paused, and drank his coffee to allow Jeff to ponder the news that he had just received. Slowly, Paul continued.

"Tyrone found out from Malcolm that Janita had loaned him the money the last time that he was late with the payment of his gambling bet. Tyrone actually thanked Malcolm for confirming his belief that Janita Morgan was a rich bitch. Tyrone also believed that Janita still owed him money because she fired him from the center. When Malcolm tried to explain to Tyrone that he could not borrow from Janita again, Tyrone told him, "Either you give me what you owe me, or I will get it from Miss Janita Morgan." Tyrone Battle hated Janita because she had 'messed up' his good thing at the center and I understand that he had vowed to pay her back. Malcolm was trying to borrow the money that he owed Tyrone from any type of finance company but before he could secure a loan, his daughter was killed and Janita was arrested for it. Jeff, my sources are reliable but they will not come forward and testify, so you must make Janita remember what actually did happen that evening. You may also be able to meet with the Chief and perhaps with what we have and what he has, we may be able to get Janita Morgan released by the weekend. That new little ex-marine policeman that works closely with the Chief did go Backatown last night and he spent a great deal of time talking to the bartender. That rookie cop may have additional information that he may share with you because the bartender would not talk to my man. The bartender claimed that everything he could say would be considered hearsay."

87

Jeff reached into his coat pocket and pulled out his cell phone and dialed Chief Ronnie Petit's office. The Chief was not in but Jeff left a voice message asking Ronnie to call him as soon as possible. When Jeff hung-up the phone, he looked at Paul and asked, "Are your men watching the policemen?"

Paul laughed and said, "Well, at that time, we really did not know that he was a policeman because he was dressed like all the other kids that live Backatown or in the hood as our young folks say today."

Jeff stared out of the glass walls for a few seconds and he slowly returned his stare to Paul's eyes. For the first time since the investigation began, Jeff was very concerned about the information that he had just received.

"Joseph Morgan's family is about to be blown apart. If Malcolm is involved in this or if his habit did cause the death of his daughter, Julie Morgan Lee's entire world will crash very shortly. She will not only have lost her daughter but she may lose her husband as well."

Paul and Jeff completed their breakfast and Paul handed Jeff a folder that contained a detailed typed report of the information that he had shared with him during breakfast.

"Jeff, I discussed the key points of our findings, but there are other areas that may be of interest to you. You may want to read the entire report before you meet with Petit."

As Paul stood up to leave he told Jeff that if he had any questions, he should call the cell phone number that was recorded on the inside cover of the folder.

Jeff thanked Paul for the information. Paul thanked Jeff for the breakfast and left the cafe.

Jeff ordered another cup of coffee and remained seated in the private booth in order to read the detailed written report.

CHAPTER EIGHTEEN

That noisy little instrument would not stop making that ringing sound.

Junior grabbed the phone and shouted, "WHAT?"

The cheerful little voice on the other end of the phone politely replied.

"What? Good morning, big brother and how are you this beautiful morning?"

"Jeanette, what do you want and why are you disturbing me so early in the morning?"

"Now, brother, don't mess with me because you know that I could have banged on your front door but I was not sure if you slept alone last night."

"Woman, mind your own business and leave my relationships alone. For your information, she left earlier this morning because she wanted to go to the gym before her work day started."

"Oh," Jeanette said, "so, you have a fitness freak this time, huh."

"I swear, I just don't understand where you women get all of that damn energy so early in the morning. Now, did you call me this early to piss me off or is there a reason for this call?"

"Wait. Wait just a damn minute. Big brother, you told me to take today off so that we could go over to Janita's place to clean up the mess."

"Oh, yes, I forgot," Junior said apologetically.

"You do realize that it'll be just the two of us because we don't want Julie anywhere near that house and we certainly don't want Pop to do it. The only other option that I can think of is to have you, my dear rich brother, pay a cleaning service."

"Huh, yeah, sure. Baby Sister you do know that there ain't nothing rich about me, comfortable perhaps, but not rich."

Junior paused for a few seconds.

"Are you sleeping?"

"No, Jeanette, I'm not sleeping. I'm just thinking, maybe we do need to hire that cleaning service because after last night I just don't feel like cleaning up anything today."

"Great," Jeanette said, "I knew that I could count on you to be lazy because I don't feel like cleaning either."

"Go to hell, Jeanette. I'll get dressed and meet you at Janita's place in about 30 minutes."

Junior hung up the telephone, picked up the remote control for the television and set the alarm to turn the television on in fifteen minutes. As Jeff snuggled under the sheets, he muttered, "Fifteen minutes more will give me that little extra energy to deal with Jeanette all day long. Junior closed his eyes and drifted off to sleep.

Jeanette hung up the phone after talking with Junior. She looked at her watch and realized that she would still have time to jog before meeting Mr. Slow Poke at Janita's house. Jeanette knew that whenever Junior estimated a time of thirty minutes, he really meant forty-five minutes so out the door and down the street Jeanette jogged.

CHAPTER
NINETEEN

As Jeff sat at the Esquire restaurant reading Paul's report, his cell phone rang. It was Ronnie Petit.

"Ronnie, thanks for calling me back. How are you? Look, man, I would like to meet with you ASAP to discuss the Morgan case."

As Ronnie looked at his calendar, he noticed Officer Franklin had placed a note regarding the Morgan case on his desk. Realizing that he needed to meet with Franklin, Ronnie informed Jeff that he would be available to meet with him in about an hour.

When the Chief hung up the phone, he immediately shouted for Franklin.

"Franklin, come in here."

While waiting for Franklin to enter the office, Ronnie began to review his notes. After a few minutes of reading, Ronnie realized that Franklin had not responded to his call. Again, he shouted for Franklin.

"Franklin, come in here."

When Franklin failed to respond, the annoyed Chief put down his notes, walked to his office door and looked around the department however, he did not see Franklin.

"Hartman, find Franklin and tell him to come to my office, now."

"Yes, sir."

As the Chief returned to his office, Hartman walked down the steps toward the Morgan's cell where Franklin was standing talking with Janita.

"George, the Chief wants you right away."

Hartman turned and walked toward the stairs but when he looked back, Franklin had not yet moved.

"George, you had better come, *now*," the irritated Hartman shouted.

Franklin immediately rushed up the steps to the Chief's office.

"Man, you better be careful and you better remember that she's an inmate."

Franklin ignored Hartman's comment and was about to enter the Chief's office when he suddenly turned and walked over to Hartman.

"Bro, thanks for the warning."

Franklin greeted the Chief and sat down. The Chief was irritated.

"You certainly took your time about getting here. I need an update regarding your investigation."

Franklin walked over to the computer and printed his investigation report for the Chief.

"When did you complete this report?"

"I prepared it last night on my home computer, following my visit to the hood, er, er, I mean Backatown and I transferred it to the department system before you arrived this morning."

The Chief thought, "these kids are going to force me to retire because I don't think that I'll ever understand computers; and I know I'll never be able to prepare a report as attractive as this one." When the Chief looked up, Franklin began to inform the Chief of his discussion with Dexter on the previous night.

"Good job, Franklin. Mr. Battle is our man but we have to prove it; we have to place him inside of that house."

"Sir, I did go down and talk with Janita to see if she could remember any visitors coming to her home that night. For some reason that evening is still a great big blur to her. Chief, we need to get Janita out of jail and I hope we can do it today."

As Franklin's voice tone changed, the Chief looked up to see what was going on with Franklin.

"Sir, I have been attracted to Janita Morgan since high school but she was so popular, I could never get the courage to tell her of my secret love for her. Now, Chief, after all these years, Janita Morgan stands so close to me, but she's still untouchable."

Ronnie stared at Franklin for a second or two and he said, "Janita has many people working to get her released from jail and I know that we'll prove that she is innocent. In fact, her lawyer, Jeff Spratt, will be arriving here shortly to discuss this case. I'm sure he has evidence that he wants to share with me in order for us to prove Janita's innocence. I'll ask Jeff to allow you to meet with us."

"Chief, I need to ask you something before her attorney arrives."

The Chief nodded his head.

"Was the little girl molested?" The chief was shocked by the question because nothing regarding molestation had been written down or discussed with anyone.

"Why do you ask that?"

"Sir, that's what's being said Backatown and I know that statement can be tracked back to Tyrone Battle."

"Well, the evidence....,"

Hartman knocked on the door to announce the arrival of Attorney Jeff Spratt. The Chief walked over to the door to greet Jeff. They shook hands and the Chief introduced Franklin to Jeff.

"So, you are the young officer that was snooping Backatown last night."

Franklin was surprised but very impressed by Jeff's comment.

"I guess Paul Mason is as good as they say. Franklin, Paul Mason is the private investigator that high priced lawyers hire to do their foot work for them."

"Not high priced lawyers, but lawyers who know that their client is innocent and want to prove it."

"I stand corrected. Jeff, will you allow Franklin to join us for this meeting in order to share details?"

"Of course, he can stay. However, we should explain to this young man, that in most murder cases this meeting would not occur. We're going to share information because I trust your boss and because *WE* are both trying to get the daughter of our dearest friend released from that little cage downstairs."

"Sir, I understand," replied Franklin.

"Paul Mason is convinced that very soon we'll be able to prove that Janita Morgan did not kill her niece."

"Franklin is also convinced that we can prove that someone other than Janita killed Amber but we must find that important missing piece that places the suspect inside of Janita's home."

As the three men sat down at the worktable in the Chief's office, Ronnie and Jeff pulled out their notes. Franklin opened the lap top computer. The two older men glanced at each other.

"Generation gap," Ronnie mumbled.

"Modern technology," Jeff replied.

The Chief opened the review session by outlining the evidence that had been established:

1. *Janita Morgan has no memory of what occurred that night.*
2. *Tyrone Battle is involved with this case.*
3. *Tyrone Battle is the creep that Janita Morgan discussed with her family.*
4. *Amber Lee was murdered and fondled.*

"WHAT?" shouted Jeff. "Are you saying that the baby was molested?"

"Someone fondled her."

"Oh my God," Jeff said. "Does Joseph know about this?"

"Joe is not aware of it. In fact, I didn't discuss this with Franklin. However, he learned about it last night because it's in the rumor mill Backatown."

"Sir, I did include that information in my notes."

"I think we should pause for a few minutes and read each other notes so that we can eliminate surprises that could delay our discussions."

Ronnie agreed. Jeff had received only two copies of the notes from Paul, so he asked to be directed to the office copy machine.

When Jeff left the office, Franklin said, "Chief, when I read your notes, I added them to our department computer. Instead of using the handwritten notes that you distributed, would you like for me to print copies of your notes for you and the Attorney?"

Overhearing the conversation as he returned to the office, Jeff smiled and said, "Ron, you better watch your back, my friend, because this young man may be your replacement when you're forced to take early retirement."

The two men laughed, and the bewildered Franklin stuttered, "Oh, no, sir, I would never do that to the Chief."

Laughing, Jeff said, "Franklin, I'm just joking."

The embarrassed Franklin smiled as he distributed his computerized notes for review. The three men sat down to read their notes.

CHAPTER
TWENTY

"Thank you, big Brother, for agreeing to pay for the cleaning service."

"Jeanette, I'm just happy that we were lucky enough to get them on such short notice."

"Lucky, hell, big brother, I have a confession to make. I think I know my big brother extremely well, so your baby sister decided to take charge of the project and I scheduled them two days ago for today."

"*You* decided to spend my money without *my* permission," Junior angrily shouted.

"No, not really," Jeanette calmly responded.

The annoyed Junior shouted, "Jeanette, you know that you don't have 'extra money' to pay for any service so how could *you* hire the service."

Jeanette really could not understand why Junior was annoyed about hiring the service that he agreed to hire today.

"You know Junior you're correct. I don't have, as you say extra money but I knew that if you would not pay for it that Pop would loan it to me if I told him why I needed it."

"Oh sure," Junior said, "a loan, huh, but just when do you plan to repay all of those other loans that all of us were stupid enough to loan you."

Jeanette smiled and said, "But, but, you all know that I do love you and one day my ship will come in and I will repay all of my debts. Junior, please stop fussing with me because I know that you're happy about not having to clean today."

"Jeanette, you have to grow up. You have to learn to budget and you have to stop depending on all of us. You know, I guess our mother knew her children quite well and that is why your inheritance from mother was not totally released to you."

Junior looked at his youngest sister and slowly he said, "Thank you for scheduling those ladies to clean for us today because I really don't feel like cleaning."

Jeanette smiled and said, "Yes, yes, I love you too. Thank you for at least admitting that you agree with my decision to utilize the cleaning service. Come Big Brother, let's go outside to the backyard and enjoy the beauty as the maids clean up Janita's house."

As the siblings entered the backyard, Jeanette said, "Janita has really tried to copy mother's backyard and she it almost duplicated it except for mother's swing. Janita's swing is okay but not as comfortable as the antique that mother and daddy found in the country."

As Junior sat on the swing, he closed his eyes and leaned his head against the swing. For the first time in several days, Junior felt totally relaxed. For a fleeting moment, he forgot about the turmoil in the family. Suddenly, the crinkle of paper aroused Junior and without opening his eyes he began to scold Jeanette again.

"Jeanette, you had better not light that damn cigarette. You know that Janita doesn't allow smoking at her house, so please don't do it when she's not at home. Woman, what's wrong with you. That's exactly what I was trying to explain to you earlier; you need to become more responsible and respect other people. You need to understand that the world doesn't revolve around you. Grow up, little girl!"

Jeanette did not like for her brother to scold her as though she was a child but she knew that he was correct *this* time. Slowly, the embarrassed Jeanette slipped the pack of cigarettes back into her pocket and quietly she sulked next to her brother on the swing.

"Jeanette, perhaps I may have spoken to you harshly but I love you. In fact, we all love you but we'd like for you to become more independent and financially more stable. You know that Pop is very concerned about you. Yes, he'll give you money whenever you need it, but Sis, try not to go there too often. He worries too much. You know what, I would like to volunteer to spend my money on you. I'll pay for your consultation fee and the first three months for you to utilize a financial planner and get your act together."

"Thanks but no thanks, my Brother. The hospital offers free financial planning as one of my benefits because I don't have to utilize the free childcare that is offered to employees with children. I have selected and registered with a financial planner. I have had my first meeting, and it is free for me because the planner bills the hospital for his services. So Bro, please tell the family that I'm growing up and becoming more independent. So, now, all I need is for everyone to love me and perhaps slip me a few bucks from time to time. Just kidding."

"Well, I guess watching *The Kendall Jackson's Self Help Show* must be beneficial to you. Thank you Kendall for encouraging my little sister to grow up or should I say, thank you Jesus for hearing the family's prayers."

"Go to hell Junior. I'm going inside to check on your Handy Dandy Maids. When I return, would you like for me to bring something for you to drink?"

"Yes, I'd like a large glass of water on the rocks and what do you mean my Handy Dandy Maids?"

"It is your money that's paying for the service," Jeanette laughed and walked up the steps through the back door.

As Junior relaxed alone in the swing, he looked around Janita's well-groomed back yard and admired how well she kept her house, inside and outside. Junior's mind drifted to his beloved mother who had not only taken care of them as children but in her will she had provided for them as adults. Junior believed most of the Morgan siblings would have eventually accumulated comfortable bank accounts sometime during their lifetime, but their mother's death insurance and other inheritance gave it to them sooner than later.

As Junior continued to admire Janita's home, he recalled how his mother had seen this old house and immediately, she saw its hidden beauty. Unfortunately, the beauty was lost in a deteriorated neighborhood that Jacquelyn Morgan believed would one day be revitalized. Jacquelyn was correct on this project and he smiled as he recalled how his mother teased his father with "I told you so." Through the years, his mother watched a once beautiful neighborhood crumble. The old wealthy owners had either died, relocated to the homes of their YUPPIE children or were residing in nursing homes. Many of the children had purchased homes in other elite neighborhoods, or relocated to other cities. Jacquelyn had envisioned the local BUPPIES rediscovering the dilapidated territory and refurbishing the once beautiful old homes. Junior remembered how his father would jokingly tell his mother that he believed she had campaigned for the mayor to recommend her ideas regarding the neighborhood so that she could say to him, "I told you so."

Later, the thirty plus professionals had done exactly what Jacquelyn had projected. The first four or five homes were sold for $1500 and now many of the homes were appraised for $500,000 or more. Of course the late purchasers had to pay much more for their run-down house because the earlier purchasers had completed their renovation projects and the value of the homes in the neighborhood increased.

Junior continued to admire his sister's house. He chuckled as he remembered the day the Morgan parents purchased the first home in that blighted neighborhood. He recalled how happy his mother was when she requested someone to walk throughout the neighborhood with her to select the "prime" piece of property. Junior recalled the good laugh that the family had at dinner one evening when Julie questioned, "prime" piece of what? Janita did agree to assist her mother with selecting the property and they eventually decided to purchase the homestead located at 123 Sherbrook Lane. Now that house was the "prime" piece of property that Jacquelyn envisioned. Janita was the only one of the Morgan children interested in the property. None of the others wanted to assist with the renovation project, so their parents decided to purchase the house in Janita's name.

Janita was very proud to be a homeowner at the age of nineteen, but Junior and his sisters often teased her about owning a piece of junk. The teasing did upset Janita when the property was first purchased but as the renovations progressed she would often say, "Just wait, I'll have the last laugh." Later, Janita reported that it took her and their mother, thirteen years, ten months, nine days and fifteen minutes to complete the reconstruction project that included the landscaping of the area immediately around the house. Looking around the property, Junior could understand when Janita proclaimed, "It was worth the wait, time and money."

Janita was always the conservative of the Morgan children. In order to be able to invest more of her money on the renovation project, she had decided with their parents' permission to reside at the family home in lieu of paying rent for an apartment. Again, Janita's siblings teased her about staying at home with "Mommy and Daddy" in order to be a homeowner of a piece of property in the slums. Junior shook his head as he looked around the piece of land that was once slum property. He whispered "This property is worth the $550,000 that an unsolicited Realtor claimed a client was offering to purchase Janita's house." Of course, Janita explained that the property would never be up for sale because she loved her home and also because it was the last big project that she and her mother worked on together. Janita truly loved her home and she worked daily to keep it beautiful. After the death of their mother, Janita had used some of her inheritance to have the entire lot landscaped. Since that initial project, Janita had done her own lawn manicuring and landscaping. Looking around Janita's yard,

Junior decided that he would also hire the landscaper to get his yard well groomed and that he would start taking more time caring for his yard.

Suddenly, Junior noticed that there was a piece of paper stuck between the windowpane and the screen in one of the upstairs windows. He wondered why Janita would place paper in the window. Junior smiled and thought, "Something is out of place. I guess Ms Neat freak is normal."

Junior's mind shifted to Jeanette and he wondered what was keeping her inside so long. He soon decided that Jeanette was probably giving orders to the house cleaners as she did to the employees at the hospital.

Junior got up from the swing and began to slowly walk around the back yard. When he again noticed that annoying paper in the window, Junior walked closer to the house and looked up at the window. He noticed that something was written on the paper. However, it was impossible to read the scribble. Realizing that he was snooping, Junior immediately looked around to make sure that Jeanette had not seen him being nosey and returned to the swing to relax. Finally, Jeanette came out of the back door with the water for him and a diet soda for her.

"What kept you so long?"

"The house cleaners or domestic engineers as they like to be called were ready to leave. However, when I inspected the house I had to point out tasks that they had failed to do well or had not cleaned at all."

"Are they gone?"

"Yep and I gave them your check that you had left on the table. Now, my brother, we have the rest of the day to do whatever you would like to do." Noticing that Junior was in deep thought, Jeanette questioned, "Big Brother, is something wrong?"

"Jeanette, what's in Janita's middle room on the second floor?"

101

"That's the guest bedroom but Janita calls it Amber's bedroom. Hey, what's that paper in the window?" Jeanette inquired.

"I don't know, but maybe we need to investigate."

"Junior, the painters who were here scraping the window casings to be painted may have left the paper in the window."

Jeanette looked at her brother and the expression of his handsome face had become serious.

"What's going on, Junior?"

Without answering her, rushing, almost running, he started to the back door of the house.

"Junior, what's wrong?"

"I don't know. I just need to check this out. Come with me."

The two siblings ran up the stairs to Amber's bedroom. The bed was located directly under the window.

"Jeanette, when I raise the window see if you can place your hand between the headboard and the mattress and pull that paper out of the window."

The startled Jeanette moved toward the bed then began to cry.

"I don't want to get on that bed because that's where Amber was killed."

"Then move," shouted Junior, "I'll do it."

Junior struggled trying to get his large hand under the headboard, but his hand would not fit.

"Okay, okay, I'll try," screamed the confused Jeanette but Junior did not hear her.

Junior raised himself off the bed and like a strong, angry man, with one mighty push, he moved the bed from in front of the window. Junior pulled the paper from the raised window and nervously opened the crumbled paper.

"Lock up the house, we've got to go."

Jeanette cried, "Junior, what's wrong?"

Junior slammed the window and ran down the steps with the crying Jeanette running behind him. Junior locked all of the doors and he and Jeanette ran out of the front door to his car in the driveway.

"Junior, where are we going?"

Junior did not answer Jeanette. However, he picked up his cell phone and dialed his Uncle Jeff's office phone number. Amy answered the phone and explained to Junior that Jeff was presently in a meeting with Ronnie Petit. Junior asked Amy for Jeff's cellular phone number and the secretary explained that her boss did not like to be interrupted when in a meeting.

"Yes, I know, but this is important so please give me his number."

Amy gave the cell phone number to Junior and he dialed Jeff's number. Immediately he heard his Uncle Jeff's voice.

"Jeff Spratt, here."

"Hello, Uncle Jeff, this is Junior and I'm leaving Janita's house. I'm on my way to see you and Uncle Ronnie."

"What do you have Junior?"

"See you shortly."

Junior disconnected the call and dialed his father's home. However, there was no answer. He immediately dialed his father's cell phone and he whispered, "Pop, please have your phone on." Within two rings Joseph Morgan said, "Hello."

"Pop, where are you?"

"I'm on my way to the office; is anything wrong, Son?"

"Pop, I'm with Jeanette and we're on our way to Uncle Ronnie's office. Will you please meet us there?"

"Yes, Son, but is anything wrong with you or Jeanette?"

"No, sir, we're both fine."

Junior wiped a tear from his eyes, and the crying Jeanette decided not to ask any additional questions. Jeanette could not remember the last time that she had seen her brother cry. When their mother died, Junior believed that he had to be strong for his sisters; therefore he mourned privately. Everyone knew that

Junior was hurting because he was truly a mother's boy and yet he never cried in front of the family. Junior and his mother had a unique relationship and he missed her immensely. Now since the murder he quietly handled the absence of Janita, his best buddy. For the first time in her life, Jeanette unselfishly realized the strength and love of her brother and she gently touched him on his arm.

"Thank you for being my brother," she whispered.

Without turning his head, Junior nodded his head and the two siblings sat in total silence as they drove to the police station.

CHAPTER
TWENTY-ONE

Joseph arrived at the police station and was told that the Chief was in a meeting. The professional Joseph Morgan politely thanked the front desk officer and walked directly into Ronnie's office. When Joseph opened the door, he saw the three men who were working on his daughter's case sitting quietly in the office.

"Have you heard from Junior?"

"Joseph, you probably received the same type of call that we received from Junior and we're waiting for his arrival," replied Ronnie.

Franklin walked out of the office and retrieved another chair. Joseph joined the other men around the table. The four men nervously waited in the office in total silence for three minutes......for six minutes......for nine minutes then suddenly the door opened

Jeanette entered the Chief's office and Junior immediately followed her. The four men could see that Jeanette had been crying but to their surprise, Junior entered the office with teary eyes. Joseph immediately rushed to his two children but Junior rushed past his father, walked over to the Chief, and handed him the piece of crumbled paper that had been located in the window.

"Release my sister, she is innocent."

The startled Jeanette cried out in pain. Her father grabbed her, led her to a chair. Then, Joseph walked over to Junior and hugged his sobbing son.

"Son, are you okay?"

Junior nodded yes and for the first time in years Joseph leaned, kissed his son on the forehead, and whispered, "Son, I love you."

Joseph returned to the Chief's table to become involved in the discussion regarding the paper that Junior had delivered to Ronnie. As Joseph looked down at the paper, he immediately recognized the writing.

"Oh, my God!"

Jeff grabbed his friend's arm and helped him to his seat. "Buddy, calm down. Can I get you something to drink?"

"I am fine. I don't need anything."

Joseph then turned to his children and asked, "Would either of you like a drink of water?" Junior and Jeanette both shook their heads. Joseph then begin to softly read the writing.

THAT MAN NAME TIRON
CAME TO MY AUNT JANITA
HOUSE. HE WANT WATER.
THE BAD MAN PUT MEDESIN
IN HER SODA ON HER TABLE.
THEN HE ASK AUNT JANITA
FOR ME. SHE ASK HIM HOW
DO YOU KNOW MY NEESE IS
HERE. MR TIRON SAID HE
KNOWS ALL THINGS. AUNT
JANITA TOLD THE MAN TO
GO BUT HE SAY WHEN HE
GET REDDE.

AUNT JANITA TOLD MR. TIRON YOU MAKE MY HEAD HERT

AUNT JANITA GOT SLEEPY. THAT BAD MAN SAID YOU BE FINE IN MOARNIN

THAT MAN IS BAD. I WILL HIDE FROM THE BAD MAN. I BETTER HIDE MY STORY THAT I RITE FOR MOMMIE.

AMBER LEE

"Oh, my God!" Jeanette cried.

"He drugged my sister," Junior shouted and that's why she can't remember what happened."

"Chief, should I bring Janita up and should we have Mr. Battle picked up for murder?" Franklin asked.

"Whoa, my man, we need to go by the book and we'll have to complete papers before Janita can be released."

"Arrest the man as soon as you can, but please don't show Amber's letter to Janita," Joseph requested.

"I agree and remember this important little letter is the only evidence that we have that places Mr. Battle inside Janita's house."

Franklin reached for the letter to file but the Chief would not release the letter.

"Franklin, I'll handle the letter and you go down and get Janita. Family, please remember that Janita will not be able to leave with you; we have procedures to follow."

Jeff said, "Joseph, don't worry, I'll take care of everything and I'll bring your daughter home after her release."

Joseph looked at his children and said, "This nightmare is about over and your sister is coming home, today."

"Joseph, where will you be this afternoon because I need to update you on some of the evidence that Paul and Ronnie shared with me?"

"When I leave here, I'm going over to meet with Julie and Malcolm."

Jeanette reminded the men in the room, "Julie will want that letter because Amber wrote the story for her."

"She won't be able to get the letter right away but I'll make sure that she receives a copy."

"We all complained," Junior said, "about Amber's habit of writing everything that we said but now we can be thankful that she acquired that habit."

The Chief asked, "Where did you two find the letter?"

"Junior found the letter in the window in Amber's room at Janita's house."

"Son, what were you doing over there?"

"Pop we had Janita's house cleaned today and now I'm very happy my baby sister convinced me to do it because we have found the real killer. Pop, your first born daughter will be coming home today."

"Hallelujah," shouted Jeanette.

"Joe, did my men return the keys to Janita's house back to the family?"

Jeff replied, "Your men did contact the family. I told Joseph that I would pick them up but I haven't done that as of yet."

Jeanette said, "Uncle Ronnie, we had Janita's house cleaned today in order to get rid of that fingerprint gook, will you have to re-fingerprint the entire house or only in areas that were missed?"

"Baby, I don't know. When the investigators read the reports, they'll make the decisions regarding the rooms to be re-fingerprinted."

"Jeanette, don't worry about the house. I'll have it re-cleaned."

"Joe, Jeanette is correct. I released the house to your family, so the police department will be responsible for having it re-cleaned."

Slowly, the door to the Chief's office opened and all eyes focused in that direction. Janita walked in and Jeanette screamed. She had not seen Janita since the day of the arrest. Sobbing the two sisters rushed to each other, and as they hugged Jeanette chattered about the events of the day. As Jeanette began to babble about Janita's upcoming release, Joseph and Junior o walked over to Janita and greeted her with hugs and kisses. Janita looked toward her Uncle Ronnie for an explanation.

"What's Jeanette babbling about? Am I being released? Am I free? Who killed Amber? Can I go home to see my sister, Julie? Am I really free?"

"Janita, you're not quite free yet. However, you will be released sometime later today because we do have another suspect."

"How can you have another suspect when the murder occurred in MY house while I was there. Who is it? How did someone get into my house? Why didn't I hear them,/him/her or whoever?

Franklin said, "Janita, our new suspect is a Tyrone Battle."

"TYRONE, TYRONE," Janita shouted. "Why would he kill our little baby, and how did he get keys to *my* house?"

"Janita, your questions will be answered very soon but I think Ronnie is eager to arrest Mr. Battle."

The Chief said, "I'm sure Franklin will be down to give you details about the investigation."

"Come, my children, let's get out of here so that Ronnie and his staff can go about their work. I want my daughter to spend this evening with her family."

"Janita," Junior said, "we'll be at Pop's place waiting for your return."

"Where is Julie and how is she doing? " Janita asked.

"She's at her place, however I'm going over there immediately after I leave here."

"Pop, please tell Julie that I've never stopped thinking about her and praying for her. Also, tell her that I've really missed her."

"Sure, baby, I will but I must leave now because I would like to tell Julie what's going on regarding the new suspect. I think I should do that before Tyrone is arrested. The news about the arrest will rapidly flow through Backatown and may also be broadcast as a news update on one of the television stations."

The Chief said, "Okay, family, say your good-byes and let us get back to what our good citizens are paying us to do. Franklin, take Janita back to her cell but I promise you will not spend another night in this place."

Janita said, "That sounds good to me" and she gave all except Franklin good-bye hugs and kisses.

"Hey," Franklin said, "what about my kiss?"

Janita smiled and said, "They're all my family."

"Oh, I need to be family before I get a kiss," Franklin mumbled as he led Janita out of the door.

Jeanette looked at her brother and whispered, "Did you see that shit? What in the hell has been going on down here in jail?"

Junior smiled and shrugged his shoulders.

"We've been worrying our asses off about our sister being in jail but she's been down here flirting and picking up policemen."

Junior began to laugh at Jeanette.

"I think I better get you out of here before you go off like some wild woman. Pop, will you call me after you leave Julie's place or when you find out the time of Janita's release?"

"Sure, Son, I'll call you as soon as I hear any news."

"Joe, don't worry about that. I'll have Amy call each of you as soon as I get word of Janita's release."

"I'm going over to Janita's place and pick up an outfit for her to wear home because it's obvious from her appearance, that the child needs some help with that hair and makeup but most of all, she also needs a new outfit."

Everyone laughed.

"Jeanette, please give my men about three hours before you go over to Janita's place. We're going to dust for additional prints in that bedroom. In fact, they should be gathering there as we speak."

The Morgan family said goodbye and left the office.

112

As the door closed, Jeff questioned the estimated time frame of Tyrone Battle's arrest.

"Don't know when we'll find that animal because people in his profession sleep in the day and do their dirty business at night. I'll give you periodic updates." Ronnie continued, "Jeff...., hm, hm, you do realize that when Tyrone Battle is arrested, he may try to implicate Joseph's son-in-law. If that happens, the Morgan family will be devastated."

"Yes, I know, Ronnie," replied Jeff, "and that's why I told Joseph that I needed to meet with him as soon as possible. Joseph will call me later today, after he visits with Julie and I'll give him the details of Paul's investigation."

Jeff extended his hand and the two friends shook hands goodbye.

CHAPTER
TWENTY-TWO

Joseph slowly walked up to the front door of Julie's house and rang the doorbell. Almost instantly, Julie opened the door and as she looked at her father, she fell into his arms and began to cry.

"Oh Pop, I hurt."

"I know baby, I know. Where is Malcolm?"

"I don't know," Julie sobbed. "I don't know and I don't care. Oh daddy, he caused it, he caused it."

"What are you talking about?" As Joseph looked inside he noticed luggage at the door. "Julie, where are you going?"

"I was on my way to your house. Pop, I have to get out of here. I have to get out of here, now."

Joseph removed his handkerchief from his pocket, wiped the tears from his daughter's eyes.

"Okay, baby, let's go."

Joseph picked up the luggage and escorted his sobbing daughter to his car.

Julie stuttered, "Pop, I can drive."

"No, you will not. Junior and I will get your car for you later."

Daddy Morgan slowly drove his sobbing daughter to his home. Joseph parked his car in the garage, opened the car door and helped Julie out of the car.

"Julie, why don't you rest for a while and we can talk later."

"Pop, I can't rest and I really do need to talk. My marriage is over. I don't have a family anymore. My baby is dead and my husband's bad habit may have caused her death."

The puzzled father questioned, "Julie, what are you talking about?"

"Daddy, Malcolm has a gambling problem. He owes a man some money, and that man called today. When I picked up the phone I heard a man say, "If you don't pay me my damn money by tomorrow morning, your wife will be next." Oh daddy, I can't believe that this is happening."

Joseph pleaded, "Julie, please sit down. I need to tell you something."

"Pop, I can't understand why this is happening to us. Oh, God, please make this hurt go away. Pop, I begged Malcolm to stop gambling. Today when I asked him about the phone call, he got mad and said I should not have been listening to his calls. I questioned him about Amber's death and he would not answer me; he ran out of the house and drove off. Now, I don't know where he is and I'm worried that he may harm that man. Then, he will be in jail with Janita."

Daddy Morgan held his daughter's hand and said, "Julie, don't worry, Malcolm will not harm the man because that man is being arrested as we speak."

The confused Julie looked at her father and said, "What are you saying? What are you talking about? Who is being arrested and for what?"

"Julie, please sit down because I need to talk with you. Baby, there is evidence that a man by the name of Tyrone Battle...."

"Tyrone!" Julie shouted. "That's the name of the man on the phone."

"Yes darling. I assumed that Tyrone was your caller."

"Did Tyrone kill Amber?"

"The police think that he did."

"Oh my God!" Julie shouted. "It's true, Malcolm is the cause of Amber's death."

Joseph held his sobbing daughter and calmly said, "Julie, Tyrone is the creep that once worked at the center and the creep that Janita saw at Clo's Hamburger Shop."

Julie sat down and in deep thought she looked at her father and asked, "So is Janita free?"

"Not yet, perhaps later today."

As tears flowed down Julie's cheeks, she said, "Thank you Jesus! Janita will be free! How did you find out about Tyrone?"

Her father pulled up a chair and sat directly in front of her and he whispered, "Amber told us."

Julie stared in shock and tears continued to roll down her cheeks.

"You know how Amber enjoyed writing what she heard. Well, Baby, she wrote what was going on in Janita's house that night and she hid the note."

"Amber. Amber. Oh Baby, I miss you so much. Daddy, I just want to hold her one more time."

"Julie, her grandmother is holding her now. Amber is being taken care of by Jacquelyn but now your mother and your daughter are worried about you."

The ringing of the phone abruptly interrupted the conversation.

"Hello." Joseph said with an obvious nervousness in his voice.

Jeanette said, "Pop, are you okay? What's going on over there? Where is Julie?"

"Julie is here with me and she's having a hard time right now."

"Daddy, ask Julie for her prescription medication and follow the dose on the bottle, but make sure it has been four hours since her last dose. I'm on my way and I should be there in about twenty minutes."

116

Joseph hung up the phone and asked Julie for the medication. He questioned the time of her last dose.

She pointed to her purse and said, "Yesterday."

Joseph walked to the kitchen for water, then he returned to the den, picked up Julie's purse and handed it to her. She opened her purse, removed the medicine bottle and took two of the pills. Her father read the label on the bottle and made a note of the time Julie was taking the pills. He re-opened the purse to drop in the medicine bottle when he noticed a small gun.

The startled father quickly asked Julie, "Why are you carrying a gun?"

"Malcolm gave it to me the day after Amber was killed."

"Do you know how to use it?"

"No, not really."

Joseph closed the purse and placed it on the table. He noticed that Julie had calmed down and had curled up on the sofa. He retrieved a blanket from the coat closet and covered his daughter. He walked over to the fireplace and lit the logs that had been stacked in the fireplace. Joseph returned to the closed purse, opened it and removed the gun. He went into his office and locked the gun in his brief case. Joseph returned to the den where he sat in his leather chair, stared at his sleeping daughter and prayed that her hurt would soon go away. Slowly, the exhausted father drifted off to sleep.

Upon Jeanette's arrival she used her door key to enter her father's home. When she found her father and sister asleep, she went into the kitchen to prepare something for the family to eat. Before starting to cook, she decided to call Junior to let him know that Julie was at their father's home and that something seemed seriously wrong. She believed it involved Malcolm.

CHAPTER
TWENTY-THREE

"Chief, they got him and they're bringing him in."

"Franklin, tell the men that I'm going to question that little bastard."

Within minutes, the handcuffed Tyrone Battle was escorted into the interrogation room. He sat on the bench next to the table and immediately declared his innocence.

"I didn't do anything. You better let me out of here. You can expect my lawyer to take legal action against you bunch of clowns."

The arresting officer closed the door and Tyrone was left alone for about five minutes as Franklin and the Chief were watching him. The Chief walked into the room and Tyrone looked up.

"Oh, I'm scared. This must be serious because I'm being questioned by the Big Man, the Chief of Police."

"Boy, shut up and speak only to answer my questions."

Tyrone, mockingly said, "Yes sir, Mister. Whatever you say, Sir."

"Mr. Battle, I know that my men read you your rights and I'm sure that they told you that we have evidence that proves you killed Amber Lee. Where were you on Friday evening?"

"If you have evidence to convict me, then why do I have to answer your goddamn questions about my whereabouts?"

"Tyrone, DO NOT curse when you are speaking with me. Now, why don't you tell me exactly what happened at Janita Morgan's house. Why did you kill Amber Lee? Boy, talk to me."

"Talk to you about what? Mr. Big Man, you suppose to know everything so why don't you tell me what you know. After all, you got me so scared, I'm shaking in my boots."

Mr. Big Man stood up. He leaned on the table directly in front of Tyrone and slowly and softly said, "We know that you murdered Amber Lee. You wiped your fingerprints from the house, but maybe you didn't do a thorough job. Maybe you missed a print or two."

For the first time, Tyrone looked at the Chief with a little concerned expression. The Chief sat down in front of Tyrone and leaned a little closer to him.

"Mr. Little Man, I know that you went into Janita's house about 9:30pm. I also know that you asked for a drink of water and I know that you dropped pills into Janita's soda while she was getting you that glass of water."

"Stop it! Stop it!" Tyrone shouted. "You're making this stuff up! How could you know something like that?"

The Chief could see the fright on Tyrone's face and he could hear the onset of panic in his voice. The Chief stood up. He began to speak louder and faster.

"Mr. Little Man, you went up those stairs and killed that little girl, then you fondled her to implicate Janita Morgan because *you* thought she was gay."

"That's not true. That's not true," Tyrone nervously shouted.

Suddenly, the Chief hit the table with such force that Tyrone and the officers observing the interrogation jumped.

He shouted, "*YOU CREEP!* How could you murder an innocent little girl and frame someone who tried to help you in the past?"

"Don't call me a creep. That's what the high and mighty Janita Morgan always called me."

"Oh…" the Chief slowly said, "…so that's what this is all about? You had problems with Janita Morgan and you framed

119

her. Why not just kill Janita? Why Amber Lee? Why a little girl?"

Trying to arouse anger in Tyrone again, the Chief said, "Mr. Little Man, you are a loser. The little girl knew you were a loser. When you pulled her from her hiding place that night she also shouted, 'leave me alone, you creep'. The Chief shouted, "You creep! You creep! You cowardly creep!"

Suddenly, Tyrone jumped up from his bench and pushed the table away from him with his handcuffed hands and he shouted, "You better leave me alone..."

"Or what?" shouted the Chief. "Now listen to me you little creep. You had better call a lawyer because you will need to decide if you want to go to trial and get death or confess and get life because I have enough on you to convict you and you know it."

The Chief turned and walked out of the room. He immediately went to the window to watch with the officers who had been observing the interrogation. Tyrone Battle stood in the center of the room, alone, just staring for about five minutes. Then, he sat on the bench and began to cry like a baby. Some of the officers watching this grown man cry turned and walked away. Franklin continued to watch as he remembered what Dexter had said about Tyrone ordering the beating of a young brother because of a gambling debt. He thought about the pictures he had seen of the little dead girl. He remembered his former classmate, Janita, sitting in jail because that animal, Tyrone Battle had framed her and, he remembered all of the people in the hood that Tyrone, an outsider in the hood, had corrupted. Dexter was correct; Tyrone Battle needed to be locked up so Franklin stared at Tyrone without any sympathy. Franklin never turned from watching Tyrone and the only words that were spoken during this waiting period were from the officer in charge of communication when he asked the Chief if he should continue to video the accused.

120

The Chief replied, "Yes, please continue because I don't want to defend accusations about our mishandling of this case."

After observing Tyrone Battle for about eight minutes the crying stopped and the Chief re-entered the room with a cell phone.

"You have one call. I hope you have a damn good lawyer," the Chief growled.

Tyrone mumbled, "I need to call my Mama."

The Chief handed the phone to Tyrone, walked out of the interrogation room and instructed the officer to stop the video and to shut off the intercom to that room.

Tyrone sat alone for five minutes, then he dialed a number. The Chief and Franklin were the only two officers still observing the pitiful Tyrone Battle. It was obvious to the observing men that Tyrone suddenly hung up the phone as it started to ring.

The Chief said, "Tyrone is having a difficult time gathering the strength to talk with his mother. It has always amazed me how hardened male criminals cannot confess their wrongdoings to their mothers. This is especially true when the boy is an only son. Those boys routinely have a strong relationship with their mothers."

As Tyrone sat in the interrogation room, he worried about what he would say to his mother regarding his problem. He dialed his mother's phone number but before it began to ring, he replaced the phone on the table. After the third attempt to dial his mother's number, Tyrone finally allowed the phone to ring.

"Hi Mom. No, I'm okay. Yes. Yes. I love you too. I guess you do know your son. Mama, remember what you have always said about my lifestyle; well, you were correct. Oh, Mama, I'm so embarrassed to have to tell you this and I'm so sorry for what you'll soon be going through. Yes. Yes, mama. No, but I'm going to be arrested for murder. I'm at the jail now. I won't tell you that mama, especially since I'm in jail. You know that they listen to everything that I say. Mom, your baby boy needed to hear your voice. Therefore, I'm using my one call to say I love you and now since I've done that I need you to contact a lawyer for me. Will you call that lawyer that we previously discussed. Mama, please remember that I love you. Yes, you can use that money for the lawyer. I've got to go now. I love you. Please stop crying. Bye, Mama."

Tyrone pressed the off button on the little cordless phone and held it for a few minutes then slowly set the phone onto the table. He sat at the table staring at the phone. Franklin and the Chief stared at him through the observation window. Suddenly, they could see his mouth moving but they could not hear what was being said.

The Chief whispered, "He has just moved into the next phase of realization and acceptance of what he has done. He could soon talk or he could wait until his lawyer arrives."

"But Chief," Franklin said. "He did not call a lawyer."

"That animal is an only child and he's smart so he did not waste his one call contacting a lawyer. He needed to hear his mother's voice, and he wanted to be the one to inform her of his present situation. His mother will take care of the lawyer."

"Mothers are always there when a child needs them, aren't they sir?"

"Yes, Franklin, especially with a son and even more so if it is an only son. Go get the phone the Chief ordered."

Franklin walked into the interrogation room. The weary Tyrone looked up.

"The Chief sent me in for the phone."

Tyrone just stared. Franklin picked up the phone and began to walk out the room.

"Yo, dude. Do I know you?"

Franklin stopped, looked back directly into Tyrone's face and said, "I don't think so."

Tyrone stared at Franklin and Franklin turned and walked away.

As the Chief watched this exchange of words through the window he suddenly noticed Tyrone's expression on his face change as though a light had been shined upon him. The Chief shouted, "Turn intercom three back on, now."

The Chief immediately heard Tyrone shout, "Negro, when I arrived at the Juke Joint the other night, you were leaving that hole in the wall."

Franklin continued to exit the room and he closed the door behind him.

"Damn, damn, damn, " Tyrone growled. " I was screwed by someone at the Juke Joint." Tyrone placed his head down on the table and waited for the cops to make the next move or until the arrival of his lawyer.

CHAPTER
TWENTY-FOUR

Not fully awake, Joseph Morgan shifted his position in his recliner. His nose was greeted by an aroma in his house that had not been present when he sat down to relax. His eyes flickered and moved to the sofa to check on his daughter, Julie, who was still asleep on the sofa under a warm blanket. Joseph thought, my nose doesn't make mistakes. I know that I smell pork chops, cabbage, and black-eyed peas. He jumped from the comfort of his chair and quietly left the den and headed directly to the kitchen. Jeanette looked up when she heard footsteps in the house and she met her father at the door, gave him a hug and a kiss on the cheek.

"Pop, how are you?"

"My belly is doing flips smelling your food. Honey, when did you get here?"

"Hours ago. And, no, I did not wake either of you because you needed the rest."

As she continued to work in the kitchen, Jeanette informed her dad that Junior had been by and they had decided to get the family and friends together to welcome Janita home.

"Baby, where is Junior, now?"

"He should be back shortly. Junior went to deliver the clothes and makeup to Janita so that she could look presentable upon her return home. You do remember how homely your daughter looked when we saw her earlier today."

When Joseph did not comment, Jeanette looked up from her cooking duties and she saw her handsome father standing, leaning on the kitchen cabinet, with his left hand above his head and smiling as he watched his baby girl work.

124

"What's up, Pop?"

Smiling, Daddy Morgan said, "I was wondering if you'd like to quit that cheap job at that hospital and come here and be my little cook."

They both laughed and Joseph said, "Baby, you are a sweet child and you have always brought so much fun into my life."

"Ah, thank you, Daddy Morgan but I bet you tell that to all of your daughters. I love you, Pop."

"I love you, too, Baby. Now, what do we have here and what can I do to help you?"

"Well, Pop, everything is under control. I'm preparing a little food for you and Julie. Melrose has been planning the gathering for later this evening to celebrate Amber's life and Janita's homecoming. Actually, she has ordered a bunch of food that Junior had agreed to purchase but Melrose said the office would take care of everything. Melrose did contact a few friends, all related to the case and they will come over later to welcome Janita home. Your son, the soon to be Ph.D., has had posters of the family made that were recommended by Olivia to help start the healing process for Julie and Janita."

"Do you think we should have folks over while Julie is still in so much pain?"

Before Jeanette could answer, Julie walked in and replied.

"Yes, Dad, we should be welcoming Janita home. She has been through hell these past few days and will have harder days ahead of her because she still hasn't had time to accept Amber's death." Julie continued, "Thanks, Pop for being here for me today."

As Joseph placed his arm around his daughter's shoulder he said, "I've been truly blessed with a beautiful, loving and caring family. I love you all very much."

Jeanette walked over and gave her sister a hug and Julie asked, "Sis, are you okay?"

125

"Of course I am but you know me, I can cry at the snap of a finger and for no reason at all."

Suddenly, the phone rang, Jeanette mumbled, "I guess it's still the youngest child's job to answer the damn phone."

"Joseph Morgan residence, Jeanette Morgan speaking."

After listening to the caller she said, "Julie, telephone, and you might want to take it in the den or living room."

Julie walked out of the kitchen and Jeanette listened for the pick up of the other phone. She hung up the phone and whispered to her father, "It's Malcolm."

Julie was on the phone for approximately ten minutes and during those ten minutes neither Jeanette nor Joseph said a word. Jeanette continued to prepare the meal and Joseph observed her as he quietly prayed for his daughter, Julie. He even talked with his dead wife during those ten long minutes. He said, "Honey, please ask God for a favor and ask him to help our hurting family."

Finally, Julie returned to the kitchen and both of the worried family members turned and anxiously walked toward her.

"I'm okay," Julie said. "When Malcolm left me earlier today, he drove around the city for an hour or so because he had decided to commit suicide. Not realizing it, he stopped in the alley near the hospital and unbeknownst to Malcolm, a physician observed him drive up and stop the car. Later, when Dr. Jarrod looked out the window, he noticed the car was still parked with the engine running. The driver was crying with a gun lying on the seat next to him. After soliciting the help of a hospital security guard, the doctor went outside to investigate the problem and trying not to startle Malcolm, he lightly tapped on the window of the car. As Malcolm reluctantly lowered the window, the hospital security guard surreptitiously opened the other door and retrieved the gun. Malcolm said, Dr. Jarrod smiled and said, "Hi friend, would you like to talk. I'm available to listen." With the help of the security guard and the physician, whom Malcolm believes was sent by God, led him crying and babbling into the hospital. After a long discussion with Dr. Jarrod, Malcolm decided to request admission into the Addictive Behavior Unit at the hospital. However, he will not be able to contact me during the first week of treatment. He is concerned about me being alone to mourn for Amber but I told him that as long as I know that he's getting help, I will be fine and as long as I'm a member of the Morgan clan, I will never be alone."

Jeanette said, "Honey child, you're right about that."

"Amen to that," Joseph added.

Junior walked into the kitchen with an arm full of goodies and said "Amen to what?"

Jeanette said, "It's about time that you brought your lazy butt back home. As in the past you have timed it perfectly, because now I'm through cooking."

Junior laughed and said, "Correct, baby girl. My daddy didn't raise a fool. Why rush back when the maid was here working?"

Julie said, "Oh Junior, don't say that."

Jeanette interrupted, "That's okay. I'll get him back. Remember brother, payback is a bitch."

Softly, Julie said, "Thank you all for being here for me during all of my hard times. Malcolm has been addicted for some time and as you know, an addiction is like any other illness that is not treated. It will tear a family apart, kill the addict or kill someone he loves. Dr Jarrod believes Malcolm's treatment may take a little longer than the average addicted patient because he has the struggle of accepting Amber's death along with the fact that he may have played a role in contributing to her death."

Joseph said, "Baby, I'm sorry and I wish that there was something that I could do to ease your pain."

"Daddy, you're right, the pain is unbearable. It feels as though someone has snatched my heart out of my chest and my entire body aches while my exhausted brain screams, Lord, please let me hold my baby one more time. And yet, I know I'm going to be okay and for the first time in months I'm beginning to see a shining light at the end of my tunnel of turmoil."

The teary eyed Joseph walked over and hugged his daughter and whispered to her, "I love you, Baby."

Realizing that the family had gotten extremely emotional as Julie explained her pain, Junior decided to share his gifts with the family. He announced, "I have a few posters I'd like to share with you. I showed them to Olivia, my favorite counselor and she believes these posters will help start the family's healing process."

Jeanette lowered the heat under her pots and all headed toward the den. Before the starving Daddy Morgan left the kitchen, he reached over and stole one of Jeanette's beautifully baked pork chops. Jeanette whispered, "Pop, you're too old to steal." He chuckled and joined the others in the den.

Junior looked at his sister, Julie and said, "What you're about to see are my favorites. I think they are beautiful and I hope that they don't make you too sad and emotional."

Junior lifted the first poster to share with the family. It was of Baby Amber with her godparents, Janita and Junior, at Amber's baptism.

"Ah, Ooh. That's beautiful."

Junior carefully turned each poster for the family to see. The next poster was of Amber taking her first step walking toward her Aunt Jeanette.

"Oh, I remember this as though it was yesterday," the crying Jeanette exclaimed.

Spontaneous laughter occurred as Junior displayed the third poster of Mama Julie, Aunt Janita, Amber and the Mighty Rat at the amusement park.

Julie whispered, "We were so happy and we all enjoyed that trip immensely. Thanks, Junior for reminding me of the happy times."

The picture selected by Junior for the next poster was of his mother, Jacquelyn, sitting on Daddy Morgan's lap and Amber sitting on her grandmother Jacquelyn's lap. The three models in this picture were all laughing and enjoying their time together.

Daddy Morgan interjected, "Now, that's a beautiful picture."

Junior said, "Amen, to that Pop. You all certainly were a handsome couple with a gorgeous granddaughter. Now, family, my stomach is growling and needs some food, so let me show you my last poster."

This poster was of Amber putting make-up on her grandmother Jacquelyn's face in front of a mirror. In the mirror you could see Julie, Janita and Jeanette laughing in the background.

"I especially like this one because I can see all of my happy girls in this poster."

Julie smiled as she looked at the pictures of her beautiful daughter and with tears flowing down her cheeks she whispered, "Thank you, Big Brother."

"It was my pleasure."

Everyone was satisfied with the posters and of course Jeanette, the emotional crybaby, left the den with tears streaming down her cheeks.

Julie said, "Please, don't drop any of your mascara laden tears into the food."

Playfully, Jeanette mumbled, "Go to hell, Julie" and she returned to the kitchen to feed her starving father.

Joseph looked at his son and said, "Those posters are beautiful, Son, and I'm sure the family will appreciate them even more as we go through the long, hard grieving and healing processes."

"That's what Olivia said and that's why she recommended that we not avoid talking about Amber."

As Joseph stared at the poster he commented on the beauty and clarity of each picture and he questioned his son regarding the final repository for the posters.

"Well, Pop, the one with Amber placing makeup on Mom has been copied for each of us but I also have five by seven prints of all of them for everyone, including Olivia."

"Junior, that's wonderful. I know everyone will appreciate the pictures. Thank you, son."

Jeanette returned to the den and announced, "Dinner is served."

Daddy Morgan responded, "At last. Thank you, Jesus. I'm starving."

Junior chimed in, "Me too. I'm so hungry that I could eat a horse."

"That's great," Jeanette interjected, "because that's exactly what we are having –horse."

They all laughed and sat down to eat. Junior lead the blessings, all said amen and the food was about to be served when the family heard the front door open.

Daddy Morgan muttered, "Damn, I'm hungry but it doesn't seem like we're going to eat tonight."

Junior got up, walked toward the door to investigate the uninvited intruders and shouted, "Looka here, looka here! Welcome Home." The entire family rushed to the living room to see Janita and to welcome her home. Janita gave her father a big hug and as she turned for the first time since Amber's funeral, she was facing her best friend, her sister, Julie. The two sisters slowly walked toward each other with tears streaming down their cheeks and embraced.

Janita sobbed, "I'm sorry, Julie. I wish I could have been here for you."

Julie sobbed, "I've missed you and I'm happy you're home."

Of course, by this time, Jeanette was also shedding tears of joy.

Junior interrupted the silence in the room when he said, "Ah, no, come on. I've had enough of this mushy stuff.

Jeanette's starting to shed those crocodile tears again. Please, can we eat?"

They all laughed, returned to the kitchen and joyfully another place was set at the table.

"How did you get home? We were expecting a call from Jeff."

"Yes, I know. I told him there was no need for him to call because Officer Franklin had agreed to bring me home."

Joseph questioned, "Isn't that the young man that helped in the investigation?"

"Yes."

"Well, why didn't you invite him in? After all, he told me that he had hoped to be seeing more of you following your release."

Jeanette said, "Big Sis, just what were you doing in that cell? Mother cautioned us to watch those quiet girls."

The bashful Janita questioned, "What do you mean, Jeanette?"

Jeanette retorted, "You're the only woman that I know who went to jail without a boyfriend and came out being escorted home by a good-looking, fine man. Now, girl, don't get cute with me because I'll put your business out in the street."

Julie shouted, "You go girl! Did you really go to jail and find a boyfriend. Girl, please don't tell me you found yourself a good looking prisoner."

Everyone laughed and sat down to eat.

Janita said, "George, who by the way, is not my man, will be over later. Amy, Uncle Jeff's secretary, invited him and Dexter, another classmate over to whatever you have planned for tonight. Janita looked around the table at her family and asked if she could say the blessing. Everyone agreed.

Junior added, "Ah man, our food will be cold by the time you stop thanking the world."

Julie said, "Junior, be quiet. Janita, you can take as long as you wish." The family held hands and Janita began her prayer

131

in thanksgiving for a loving and caring family who with God's help had found evidence to have her released. She also asked for strength for Julie to be able to function during the time when loneliness for Amber seemed unbearable. Junior cleared his throat and Janita ended her prayer with a thank you for the food and protection for the family when eating the food that was cooked by their sister, Jeanette.

When the prayer finally ended, Junior reached over, picked up a casserole dish and said, "Let's eat."

Conversation and love were experienced throughout the meal; however, at one point the discussion became extremely emotional. The Morgan siblings could see that their father was holding back tears and as they tried to cheer him, somberly, Joseph whispered, "I'm missing your mom and I wish she could be sharing this dinner with us."

Julie softly said, "Daddy, I understand because I wish that my Amber could also be here with us, but they can't and we hurt. But, Pop, you and mom taught us that the family's love and commitment would help us through these hard times. And, I believe that."

Daddy Morgan said, "Thank you, Julie. For a moment, I forgot. Now, kids, I do have a request. I would like for all of my children to sleep here tonight. I really need you and it'll be comforting to me to know that my children are here, safe in my home."

Junior said, "No problem, Pop. I think we all need each other tonight and I too want to make sure that my sisters are safe and will have a good night's sleep for the first time in awhile."

Suddenly, to everyone's surprise, Jeanette tapped on her glass with her spoon and said, "May I have your attention, please. I, too, have a request."

At this time, all eyes focused on the comical, fun-loving Jeanette and all wondered what words would were about to come out of their youngest sister's mouth.

"I would like for all of the pigs who consumed my delicious food to get off of their butts and help clean up this filthy ass kitchen that the neophyte cook messed up."

All laughed.

Junior replied, "No problem, baby girl. I'm sure that you ladies have so much gossip to share with each other, I'll remove all the trash. Then Pop and I will give you your privacy to catch up on the news."

"Junior, no matter what happens in this family, we can count on you to run from work."

Julie agreed with Janita, then turned to Jeanette and said, "Jeanette, your food was delicious and I thank you for being here for me."

Jeanette smiled at her sister and in response to Julie's statement, she began to sing *Family* by Thomasina Clarke and the others joined her.

The kitchen had been cleaned, the trash had been taken out, the "juicy" gossip had been shared among sisters, the fire had been re-kindled, and calmness had returned to the house. Joseph looked around his full house and remembered how bleak yesterday seemed and how vibrant today had become. He announced to the family that he was going to sixty-thirty Mass and would be back shortly.

"I'm going with Pop," said Janita.

"So am I," said Julie.

Jeanette said, "Please, pray for me."

Junior looked up from the magazine and realized the family was waiting for him to say if he would be attending mass with them. "Oh, um, tell my good Buddy, Jesus, that I'll see him later."

Daddy Morgan shook his head as his two children made excuses for not going to church. "Two peas in a pod," he whispered as he ushered Julie and Janita out the door.

Following the departure of the group, Junior requested Jeanette's assistance to hang up the posters of Amber. As they worked, Jeanette updated Junior about Malcolm's gambling addiction and also his involvement with Tyrone.

Jeanette added, "Malcolm seems to be on his way to recovery because he has checked himself into the Addiction Behavior Unit at the Allen Lemon Rehabilitation Facility."

Junior frowned and said, "I'm happy that Malcolm has made a decision to seek help. I hope this isn't another of his ploys to get sympathy and money from Julie. You know, for the first time since I've known Malcolm, the last time I saw him I wanted to beat the hell out of him. I didn't like the way he was treating my sister and I wanted to encourage her to leave him but I knew Julie had to make that decision. I honestly do hope that this treatment is successful because I will not sit back ever again and watch him hurt her."

"Junior, don't worry. Malcolm's treatment is going to be successful because the others will pray it successful. Big Bro, I think we really need to start going to church."

"Yeah, yeah, I guess you're right. Okay, I'll start going to church. We can start last week."

"Ah, Junior, I'm serious."

"I bet you're serious, but you need to be careful about that church stuff because if you and I both start going to mass again, Pop will probably have a heart attack. Now, do you really want that on your conscience."

Suddenly, the doorbell rang and Jeanette said, "We finished that task just in time." The two siblings walked to the front door to greet the visitor.

"Come in and welcome to Daddy's home."

Amy, Melrose and Kristi , an employee from Earnestine's Catering Service walked into the house.

Junior said, "Melrose, thank you for planning this evening for the family. Just let us know what we can do to help."

Melrose planned the evening and Earnestine's Catering prepared the food. We all have assignments and everything should be set up in twenty minutes."

Jeanette snapped her finger and said, "You go girl, the house is yours. Do your thing." Melrose immediately began to give orders and within minutes, Joseph Morgan's living room had been beautifully transformed for gathering.

Olivia Jenkins was the first guest to arrive. Junior met her at the door, thanked her for her counseling recommendations and for managing the Center during Janita's absence.

"Joseph Junior, you don't have to thank me for doing things for and with the family that I've adopted and truly love."

Jeanette quickly turned and said, "Mrs. Olivia Jenkins. "Hello. I haven't heard anyone call Junior, Joseph Junior since our mother died. How are you? Are you sure you adopted the Morgan family or did the Morgan family adopt you?"

Olivia laughed as she hugged Jeanette and said, "It doesn't matter who did the adoption, I'm happy we're family. How are you?"

"I'm doing fine. In fact, we were all fine until we lost our little baby. Things were really rough for awhile but I think we're beginning to heal. Julie is still having a difficult time. However, the family will help her except for the pain in our hearts for Amber."

Olivia asked, "Where is Julie?"

"She went to Mass with Pop and Janita. They should be returning home very shortly."

The back doorbell rang and Jeff Spratt and his wife Paula entered through the kitchen door.

"We know that's long time family members because most people don't even know we have a back door."

Paula walked in, greeted the guests and kissed Junior and Jeanette.

Jeff said, "Yep, we're family and we walked through the private path between our yards because we, no, *I*, needed the exercise."

Paula walked over to the dining room table and said, "Jeanette, your buffet table looks great."

135

"Honey child, that's Melrose and Amy's table and I agree that the table looks gorgeous and the food delicious."

Without being noticed, the churchgoers entered the house through the den entrance. For the first time, Janita spotted the posters of Amber that Junior had hung around the wall.

"Oh, no!" Janita sobbed. Julie walked over and hugged her sister and the two sisters began to cry.

Olivia motioned for the guests to remain in the living room and she went into the den to assist Daddy Morgan in his attempt to comfort his daughters.

Olivia whispered, "It's okay to cry, let it out. Amber is in heaven with her grandmother and she's as happy now as she is in that picture on the wall."

As the two sisters admired the pictures, Olivia moved over to stand at Joseph's side. Olivia whispered, "That's a beautiful picture of my friend, Jacquelyn. She looks so pretty and happy."

"Yes, I too love that poster. Junior had copies of that picture of Amber and Jacquelyn made for all of us."

"I certainly hope that he included me as a family member because I would like to receive a copy."

As Olivia whispered about the pictures, Janita and Julie stopped crying and begin to admire the pictures. They slowly walked in front of each poster and remembered the occasion when each picture was taken and they shared the memories with their father and Olivia, their mother's best friend. During this private time Jeanette kept peeping into the room yearning to become part of the moment. However, her father requested that they be given a few additional minutes to reminisce.

Upon the arrival of the "good looking" policeman, Jeanette could no longer control her desire to barge into the den. Slowly she opened the door to the den and when she heard laughter, the happy-go-lucky Jeanette entered the room.

"How dare you have a party in here and not include me. Remember, I'm the baby, not the middle child, so don't treat me like a stepchild." Jeanette jokingly continued, "Girl, you better come out of this room before I snatch your new good-looking boyfriend that just walked into the house."

"Jeanette, what are you talking about?"

"Girl, don't play innocent with me. You know I'm talking about Franklin."

Julie asked, "Who is Franklin?"

Jeanette quickly responded, "When we were out here all worried and praying about Janita being in jail, our sister was in jail flirting with the cops and now one of them is here to see her."

Daddy Morgan added, "And we all know that if Jeanette was praying because Janita was in jail, she had to be worried and scared."

They all laughed.

Olivia said, "Let's go out and meet Janita's young man."

"But he is not *MY* young man."

"Great," Jeanette said, "I'll take him."

As Olivia and Joseph left the room, Olivia commented to Joseph, "You'll still have some bad moments with the girls but with the love that your family share, you'll be able to survive this ordeal. You know Joe, your children genuinely love each other. That's important and you should be proud."

"I am. I'm proud and I'm blessed."

The two old friends left the den and joined the other guests to celebrate the return of Janita, his first-born daughter. Joseph walked toward Melrose to thank her for her assistance and loyalty during his family's time of trouble.

"Melrose, I know that planning this gathering is not part of your job duties but I do appreciate all that you've done for me and my family."

"Boss, I'm only doing what you pay me to do because my job description says any duty that's assigned or required by the supervisor."

They both laughed.

137

Overhearing the conversation, Jeff joked, "Little lady, I do hope that doesn't mean that you're on the clock tonight because if you are, Amy will assume that she is also on the clock."

"No, no. I don't expect to be paid for tonight."

"Melrose, you had better speak for yourself because I expect my boss to pay me for my after hours work." They all laughed and the two secretaries walked away and the two best friends shook hands.

Joseph said, "Thank you, my friend, and please send me your bill."

"Sorry, Joe but I don't work for you. Your daughter hired me and she and I have discussed my fees. But you know, according to some of my other clients, my bills get lost in the mail."

Looking toward Janita, Jeff said, "Joe, from the look in Franklin eyes as he talks with your daughter, you may be gaining a new son in the not too distant future."

"You may be right. Take a look at that silly expression on Janita's face. Now, I'm getting like Jeanette. I too question what in the hell went on down there in jail?"

As the Chief walked up, he overheard Joe's comment and he questioned, "What do you think went on in my jail?"

The men laughed at Ronnie defending his police department.

"How are you two doing?"

"I'm elated to have Janita's case closed."

Joseph said, " Amen to that. You know, it is hard for me to believe that someone Jacquelyn and Olivia brought into our family business killed my granddaughter and then tried to frame my daughter for the crime."

Jeff said, "I had a very interesting call from Mrs. Battle, Tyrone's mother."

"Oh really." Joseph said. "And does she want you to represent her son?"

"Yes, she does. She lives out of town and she has no idea of my relationship with the Morgan family. The poor woman just wants her son out of jail. Of course, she said what every parent says whenever a child gets into any type of trouble: my son is innocent, my son is being framed, my son could never hurt a child and my son could never commit such a crime."

Joseph stared, almost speechless, then he whispered, "Those are the words that I said when Janita was arrested. Sometimes, my friend, those words are true."

Suddenly, Franklin walked over to the three friends and he whispered to the Chief, "Sir, according to Dexter the folks in the hood are saying the hit men that worked for Tyrone's boss killed the little girl."

"Thanks, George, but remember, tonight you are off duty having a great evening with a beautiful young lady that you've been secretly in love with since high school."

"Chief," George shouted, "You're embarrassing me and furthermore you don't have to tell the whole world about my feelings for Janita."

"George you couldn't have fallen for a nicer lady but I agree with your Chief, go and enjoy this beautiful evening."

After George walked away, Jeff and Joseph simultaneously said, "Could this be true?"

"For the love of me, I just can't figure out how the people Backatown get any and all information before anyone else in the city; and, most of the time, their gossip is more accurate than the local newspaper."

"Are you saying that the Backatown rumor is correct? Is Tyrone innocent?"

"Wait. Wait. Slow down," Ronnie begged. "Our investigation will establish what's true and what's gossip."

"If Tyrone didn't do it then there were other people in my daughter's home. Is her home not safe anymore?"

"My friends, I think we need to delay all of our discussion until later because we are standing in the middle of a…"

"Celebration," Junior added, and I agree, this room is not the place for this discussion so why don't you all move into Pop's office."

"Can't this wait until tomorrow?"

"No," Joseph said, "my daughter will be returning to her home and we need to know if there's any danger before she returns home."

"Ronnie, please tell us what is going on."

"There's nothing much I can tell you."

Annoyed, Junior snapped, "Why not let us decide the importance of the little bit that you do know or, do you think I should drive to the hood and find out what's going on in your office?"

Ron snarled, "Cool it young man. Now, do you understand why I didn't want to discuss this tonight?"

Joseph instructed his son to calm down as he escorted the three men into his office. As the four men reached Joseph's office, quietly they waited, and then the Chief began to update the men.

"Did Tyrone talk to you or anyone about the case?"

"Is that a question from Janita's lawyer or from Tyrone's future lawyer?"

"Man, you know that I would never involve you or your actions in my cases, especially when we're talking off the record. And, for your information, I did not accept Tyrone's case. I referred Mrs. Battle to my former classmate, Attorney Shirley Eustace."

Joseph said, "Oh, hell, stop this shit. This case is just about over and we'd better not let the actions of Tyrone Battle jeopardize our long-term friendship."

In shock, watching the interactions of his Dad and friends, Junior attempted to ease the tension in the room. Junior

140

said "Whoa, I must be a man now because my Pop's friends are acting up in front of me. In fact, you're acting like me and my friends."

The three friends looked at each other and shouted, "Shut up Junior."

Jeff continued, "Junior, you're getting too smart for your own drawers."

As the group sat down, Jeff and Junior began to laugh at the confrontation that had just occurred and the emotions of all begin to calm down.

"Okay, gentlemen, I'll try again to briefly explain the evidence in the case, some of which came from Paul Mason's investigation for Jeff, the investigation by Franklin, the letter that was written by our little victim and finally the review and analysis by other officers. Jeff, please add your two cents whenever you feel it's needed."

"First of all, an eye witness saw Tyrone's old Mustang circling the block several times in front of Janita's house.

Tyrone parked his car in front of Nays' Deli located on the corner near Janita's house. Several people noticed the car because it's a beautiful well kept antique. The little creep used the telephone book in Nays to confirm Janita's address because we found his fingerprints on page 157 near J.A. Morgan at 123 Sherbrook Lane."

"That's Janita's address," Junior whispered.

"Yes, it is and I asked Tyrone to write 123 on a piece of paper and it's almost identical to the imprint that was left in the phone book."

"Ron, I am impressed with your officer's work."

"What do you mean, my friend? Are you saying, that you thought my officers are incompetent?"

"No." Jeff laughed. "I'm commenting about the details that your men discovered."

"Well, yes, " Ronnie continued "that's what happens in an investigation; details are discovered."

Trying to calm the tone of the discussion, Joseph questioned, "Ron, what else did you find?"

"Tyrone or his helpers tried to wipe the apartment clean of his fingerprints, however, we were able to pick up his left thumb print on the casing of the front door near the doorbell. That clue led us to believe that our man was left handed."

"Is Tyrone left handed?"

"Yes, Junior, he is. However, all of the evidence that we had catalogued from our entire investigation could not trigger an arrest because we could not place Tyrone inside of Janita's home. Then, thanks to the discovery of the letter, our little Amber spoke to us via her story that she wrote for her mommy. Amber placed Tyrone inside of Janita's house."

"Ronnie," Jeff questioned, "Other than the letter, were you able to actually place Tyrone inside the house?"

"Today, after the discovery of the letter, my men went back to Janita's house to search for Amber's hiding place."

Joseph's mind drifted for a moment from the discussion, then staring directly at the Chief, his deep baritone voice slowly asked, "Where did she hide?"

"Exactly where all kids her age hide; under the bed that is located under the window where Junior found the letter."

"So, that's how Amber was able to stick the paper in that window. I could not figure it out because it was hard for Jeanette and me to pull the paper out of the window. I contributed my difficulties to having large hands."

"Junior, you're correct. Amber stuck her letter in the window when she was hiding under the bed. After the discovery of the letter, I questioned Janita about the window being opened. She remembered opening the window earlier to allow fresh air to circulate in the room before Amber's bedtime. Janita was able to recall that incident because it occurred prior to her being drugged by that damn animal."

With the six eyes and ears focused on him, the Chief leaned back in his chair and rested his head against the wall and proudly continued his briefing,

"Now, to go back to Jeff's question regarding other evidence that placed Tyrone inside the house. When searching for Amber, Tyrone identified the room because he found Amber's luggage and toys in that room so he searched there for her. Sometime in the search, he realized that the window was open and to eliminate a scream or any type of noise to alert the neighbors or a passerby, he closed the window. But he obviously forgot about the window closing and during the process of wiping off fingerprints, the goons failed to wipe off the window and now we have Tyrone's fingerprints in that upstairs bedroom."

"Tyrone Battle is guilty, even if he didn't actually do the killing. That bastard IS guilty," Jeff announced.

Junior asked, "How was she killed?"

"The bastard as Jeff correctly identified him, is a coward. He is a weak SOB but thanks to his cowardice he could not let her suffer. He dragged her from under the bed by her ankles..."

Suddenly, the door of Joseph's office was jerked open and the four startled men looked back.

"Chief, wait. We've been listening to you from the intercom that was somehow turned on during your discussion."

"Oh shit," the Chief said.

Joseph rushed toward his sobbing daughters, he pointed to the intercom switch that Ron had inadvertently activated when he leaned back in his chair with his head resting on the wall.

"Franklin, why in the hell didn't you tell me earlier. We'll have to discuss this later in the office."

Jeanette snapped, "This isn't his fault. Julie and Janita begged him not to alert you because they couldn't wait until trial to learn what happened in that house that night."

"We needed to know," Janita sobbed.

Pulling away from her father's arms with tears flowing from her eyes, Julie walked over to the Chief, looked him in his eyes and whispered, "Uncle Ron, how was my baby killed?"

"Baby, she did not suffer. According to the coroner, he gave her a glass of punch that he had laced with a large dose of sleeping pills that immediately put her to sleep."

"Did the pills kill her?"

Hesitantly, the Chief carefully responded, "Honey, they choked her."

"Oh my, God," Jeanette screamed and she began to cry.

As Dexter walked over to console Jeanette, he said, "Chief, in the hood, they're saying the marks on the little girl's neck were too large to be Tyrone's hand. Some folks are saying that the prints belong to one of the two dudes who routinely beat up on people with over due gambling debts."

"It's still a rumor, son. However, you and I both know that rumors Backatown are often correct."

Jeff added, "That would explain how a little league hustler like Tyrone could wipe an entire house of all evidence. That was the piece of the puzzle that just didn't fit. I didn't think that Tyrone was capable of removing every single print."

"That issue also bothered me and my other officers working on this case. It was too clean. If those criminals had known that the window had been opened, I'm sure those professional hoodlums would have wiped off the one fingerprint that placed Tyrone in that house."

Dexter said, "Chief, the people in my neighborhood would like to get all three killers off the street."

"Please tell our families Backatown that we'll get them off the street and securely behind bars. That's a promise."

Joseph said, "We've heard enough."

Olivia added, "It's time to eat some of the delicious food that has been prepared for us."

Joseph ushered everyone out of his office to the living room.

144

CHAPTER
TWENTY-SIX

At six-thirty, as the Chief stretched to begin his morning jog around the track, Franklin, who had already jogged four miles, ran up to him.

"Good morning."

"Why are you jogging over here this morning?"

"Well, Dexter asked me where could the three of us meet away from the precinct so I recommended that we meet this morning before you start your daily jog."

"Dexter doesn't look like a jogger to me."

A voice from a distance replied, "Sir, you're correct. Jogging is for you old dudes. I am a gym man. Weight lifting is my thing. Good morning, sir."

Dexter shook the Chief's hand. He handed the Chief a small gym bag.

"You might find this helpful in your investigation."

The Chief looked into the bag that contained two plastic bags and in each bag was a crushed beer can.

"What's this, son?"

"For almost a year, I've watched a brother and two white dudes mistreat my people. Every time a crime occurred there were no fingerprints. Everything had been wiped clean. One evening, those hoodlums waited for a truck driver because he was behind on payments for his gambling losses. I was the bartender at the Juke Joint and I offered them a beer on the house. No beer head turns down a free beer. They drank their

beer, squashed their cans as they routinely do and were about to
place them in their pockets to take the cans with them when the
truck driver walked into the bar. The truck driver recognized
them and begun to run. I immediately placed the squashed beer
cans into the plastic bags to store for future use. Later, I stored
the cans in my gym locker in a pair of dirty old shoes. Sir,
hopefully, the fingerprints on these cans will help you get a
conviction. Chief, those dudes will remember the incident
because after they beat up the truck driver they came back to get
the cans. I apologized and explained that I thought they were for
the trash. I showed them the pile of old beer cans and even
offered to pay them to remove all the cans. Of course, they
declined the offer."

"Son, thank you. If you think you'll need protection or if
we need to talk to the owner of the bar where you work, I'll
personally contact him."

"Oh, no," Franklin said, "Sir, he's the owner of the bar."

The surprised Chief said, "Great. Dexter my offer still
stands. If you think that you will need protection we could
arrange for you to take a vacation."

Dexter laughed and said, "I'll take you up on that offer
but only if you can arrange to have that pretty little Jeanette
Morgan take the trip with me."

"Sorry man, you're on your own with trying to seduce
Jeanette. However, if she decides she's interested in you, you'll
know immediately. However, at that point you won't know who
is the seducer, you or Jeanette. She's *not* shy or quiet as the other
sisters. She's different but I think you'll like her."

"Once again, thank you, son. I don't think I'm going to
jog today. I'm going into the office in hopes to finally identify
fingerprints. Good-bye, Son. Franklin, I'll see you later."

Franklin said, "Dexter, I'm so proud of you and I thank
you for your help on this case. By the way, Janita mentioned to
me last night that she thought Jeanette might be interested in you.
Janita recommends that you not call Jeanette for two to three

days.   She thinks you should let Jeanette wonder if you're interested in her."

Dexter laughed and said, "That sounds extremely mean to me. What do they think will happen if she knows, today, that I'm interested in her?"

"Bro, I don't know but I bet you can handle her."

"Thanks, man, for the vote of confidence. I've got to go, now. Keep me posted on the investigation."

"You know I'll keep you posted. I had not planned on going into the office today but I'm going to check with the Chief regarding his findings."

The two buddies shook hands goodbye.

CHAPTER
TWENTY-SEVEN

On Saturday morning, Joseph Morgan walked into his den and found Julie sleeping on the sofa in front of the posters of her daughter. Trying not to disturb her, quietly he backed out of the room. He sat down at the kitchen table and opened the newspaper but before he could begin to read Julie walked into the kitchen.

"Good morning, Pop. Would you like to take a ride with me?"

"Of course, I'll ride with you but where are we going?"

"To see Amber and mother."

"I had also planned on going to the graveyard later today, so I'm ready whenever you are."

"Pop, can we go now?"

"Of course we can."

Joseph wrote a note to his other children informing them of his destination and he led his daughter out the door.

Janita entered the kitchen to get a glass of grapefruit juice and she noticed the note from their father. Realizing that her father and Julie would be gone for most of the morning, Janita decided to go to the center. She added her destination to her father's note because she would have to drive either Junior's or Jeanette's car. She decided to use Jeanette's car because Jeanette would probably be sleeping most of the day. While driving to the center she clicked the radio on and to her disgust, the local news reporter was discussing her release and Tyrone's arrest.

She immediately turned the station to the "oldie but goodie" radio station and *Thanks for Last Night* by Frankie Martin, a local artist, began to blast through Jeanette's powerful new speakers. Janita's thoughts immediately drifted to George Franklin and in her heart she began to secretly hope that George would become more than a former classmate to her. Suddenly, a horn from a passing car blew and her attention immediately returned to her driving. Realizing she had momentarily veered into the other lane, she lowered the radio and tried not to think about that gorgeous Mr. Franklin. Upon her arrival at the Center, she noticed Olivia's car and by the time she reached the front door, Olivia had opened it for her to enter.

"Welcome back, boss. I expected you to come here this morning so I decided to arrive earlier than you to try to organize your pending file."

"Thank you, Olivia, but I didn't expect you to do everything alone. I'm so appreciative of your support during this ordeal. You, and you alone, kept the center open. I owe you, my friend."

"You don't owe me anything. We're both here because we both love this center and we both want your mother's dream to succeed. Now, let's have a cup of coffee and get to work."

CHAPTER
TWENTY-EIGHT

George Franklin entered the Chief's office and asked, "Any news yet?"

"No, not from the analysis on the cans, but two other sets of finger prints were located in Janita's house. It seems as though two people were looking under the bed on opposite sides. The outsides of the bed railings were clean. However, on the inside of the railings we picked up clear prints and I'm hoping those prints match the prints on Dexter's beer cans. If they match, we'll be able to remove three hoodlums off the street."

"Sir, when we get them behind bars, the prayers from so many of the people in the hood will be answered."

"Franklin, your friend Dexter, seems genuinely concerned about people and the crime in his neighborhood."

"Yes, sir, he's a good man and is really very involved with the politics in that area. The senior citizens usually contact him for assistance instead of their elected officials. Many of them have encouraged Dexter to run for an office but he prefers to be in the background. He owns the Juke Joint Bar but everyone believes he is the bartender. He also owns the Ebony apartments but they're being managed by a nice young couple that was evicted from their previous home when the glass company downsized and both were laid off. The young couple keeps the apartments in tiptop shape and there's a waiting list of people trying to rent an apartment. I guess if the folks Backatown knew that Dexter owned the Ebony apartments, they would be hounding him day and night for special favors. He owns stock and has an extensive portfolio. In fact, when I was in the military, monthly, I sent money home to my parents' to help them with their bills but they deposited the money in a regular savings account. They wanted to make sure that upon my return home, I would have the money for a deposit on a house or could pay cash for a car. One day, Dexter visited with my parents and upon his departure, mom asked him to make a deposit into the savings account. He did make the deposit, however on his next visit he brought them basic investment books designed for senior citizens. After my mother read the books, she called him and he helped her invest the money. When I came home, my mother proudly presented me with the monthly report of her investments, and I was shocked how the money had grown. Sir, I didn't know that Dexter was the dude that helped my parents until this week when I mentioned to mom that I had seen him. At that time, she told me Dexter was the one who helped her with the investments. Dexter is a self taught intelligent man and I certainly hope he can find a nice girl to marry."

"Son, perhaps he did find her last night. He did seem very interested in Jeanette Morgan."

"Yeah, I think that would be great."

"Do you know what will be great about this situation?"

"Two nice people will find each other."

"Yes, but that's not what I was thinking about. Jeanette thinks Dexter is a bartender and if she becomes interested in him, she'll be surprised at what he has to offer her."

The ring of the phone interrupted the conversation.

"Chief Petit here. Yes. Yes. Great job. Thanks. I will have Officer Franklin pick up the written reports. Once again, thank you."

The Chief hung up the phone and said, "We got a match. Your friend, Dexter, knew the law. He labeled each beer can with each drinker's name. He documented the date and time of the occurrence and he had two witnesses sign the label. One of the witnesses was the policeman on duty making rounds at the time and the other was a lawyer who was in the bar meeting a client. The policeman wrote a report and he detailed their actions."

"Wow, so, Dexter had everything witnessed and legally marked to help us clean up the hood."

The Chief ordered, "Franklin, have the men pick up those two criminals, Adams and Fitzgerald for murder one."

The Chief slammed his hand against the desk and shouted, "We got them! We got them!"

As the two men thought about the pending arrest of Adams and Fitzgerald, a silence was instilled in the office. The Chief and Franklin sat staring into space, then, the Chief spoke.

"George, before you leave; do you have Dexter's phone number? Immediately, after we pick up those criminals I would like to personally thank Dexter."

"Thank you for taking the time to call him. I know Dexter will appreciate your call."

"Please remind the men to be careful. Adams and Fitzgerald will be carrying guns. I want them alive and I don't want to lose any of our policemen."

"I'll get Dexter's phone number for you."

CHAPTER
TWENTY-NINE

"Janita, I think we've worked long enough for your first day back and there's someplace that I think you need to go and I would like to be the one to go with you."

"Where are we going?"

"Janita, you need to go back into your home and perhaps today is the right time to do so. I don't think you have to spend the night but I do think you should visit. "Do you have a key to your house with you?"

Janita glanced at Jeanette's keys and noticed that her door key was still on Jeanette's chain. Janita nodded her head.

"Yes, I have a key."

As she agreed to go with Olivia, tears began to form in her eyes. Olivia offered to drive her but Janita decided that they should go in separate cars. When Janita arrived home, Olivia was already sitting on Janita's front steps awaiting her arrival. Without saying a word to each other, Janita opened the door and the two ladies walked into the house. As Olivia stood in silence, Janita walked through the entire house, except for Amber's bedroom. She returned to the master bedroom, removed a few clothes from her closet and began to pack clothes to take with her to her father's home.

As Olivia observed Janita's action, she slowly walked over to Janita, took her hand and said, "Little lady, you have to go into that room. Please, go now."

"Olivia, I'm not sure I'm ready to go into that room."

"Okay, Baby. Let me know when you're ready. I'll be here for you."

Olivia walked into the hallway and quietly waited.

A little later, Janita walked toward Amber's bedroom. She opened the door, and slowly walked around the room. Sobbing, she walked toward the bed. She touched the bed, and lovingly stroked the mattress. Janita lowered her body to sit at the foot of the bed. Crying uncontrollably her flaccid body slid down to the floor on the side of the bed. Janita cried out for Amber.

"Amber! I love you so much and I miss you. Amber, I'm sorry. I'm so sorry for not protecting you. Baby, I miss you. Oh, God, I loved her so much. God, You should have taken me and left our precious angel here. Now, God, You need to come here and ease my pain. It hurts. It hurts. It hurts so.....much...."

Olivia walked into the bedroom, sat on the floor next to Janita, stroked her hair and whispered, "Let it out baby. You'll feel better. Let it out."

Janita continued to cry and talking to Amber. As the sobs weakened, Olivia helped Janita lift her drained body to the bed and when she could cry no more, she drifted off to sleep.

The teary eyed Olivia walked downstairs, opened a can of beer, walked out the back door and in deep thought, sat in the swing to wait for Janita to wake.

About an hour later, Janita opened her eyes, stared for a few minutes then she lifted herself from the bed. Like a wild woman, she stripped the linen from the bed and removed the curtains from the window. She rushed downstairs to the back door and pitched everything into the yard. Without commenting, Olivia watched as Janita continued to throw out articles that decorated Amber's room. When the disposal of items stopped, Olivia walked over to Janita's pile of trash and began to retrieve paraphernalia that she felt Janita might later regret discarding.

Trying to compose herself, Janita walked out of Amber's room, closed the door behind her and entered her bedroom. Walking in front of her dresser, she caught a glimpse of her face in the mirror and the energized Janita rushed into the bathroom. She washed her face, replaced her makeup and packed the rest of the items to take with her to her father's home. As Janita walked passed the window, she realized that she had forgotten that Olivia was still at the house with her. She waved to Olivia, picked up her luggage, walked downstairs and out the back door.

Without turning to look at Janita, Olivia said, "Your Mom is all around this yard and it was nice being out here to talk with my friend." Olivia lifted her middle-aged body from the swing and proclaimed, "Great imitation of Jacquelyn's swing, but not as comfortable. Are you ready, baby?"

"Yes, let's go."

"I'll see you Monday morning."

"Thank you for being here today."

The ladies got into their cars and drove off in opposite directions.

CHAPTER
THIRTY

When Julie and Daddy Morgan returned home from their visit to the graveyard, Junior and Jeanette were still asleep.

"I'll never understand how those two can sleep so long."

Daddy Morgan, laughed and said, "Your mother claimed they inherited that from me."

"You?"

"Yes, baby in my younger days, I could and I did do the same thing. As I aged, my sleeping patterns changed."

"So, that's why you never got upset with them."

"Yes, I understand them because I was a late sleeper."

"Pop, please excuse me for a few minutes so that I can check my e-mail."

Julie retrieved her messages and as she had hoped, she did have an e-mail from Malcolm. Her heart began to pound rapidly. She immediately opened his note.

Hi Honey.

I'm not breaking the rules. They said no phone calls and when I reviewed the rules, they didn't say that I couldn't use e-mail. I'm writing to apologize to you again and to tell you that I love you. I miss you and Amber and my heart hurts for you and our daughter. I may not always tell you and at times I'm a little jealous about it, but you have a wonderful family. Junior talked with the supervisor on duty, Mrs. Nattie Green, and she allowed a five-minute visit. Junior brought me a poster of you and Amber. It now hangs in my room. Honey, I wish I could be with you as we grieve for Amber but we both know that wouldn't be good for us at this time. I love you. /Malcolm

Julie re-read Malcolm's email and she replied:

Hi Babe: I love you and will be waiting for you with open arms. I'm okay but the pain for our daughter is often unbearable. I'm thankful to dad for having the entire family at his house. It feels good to be with them. Get well soon. I love you.

Julie returned to the kitchen where her dad had pulled out some of the food from the previous night and they began to have lunch. Like always, Junior and Jeanette smelled the food warming and they both entered the kitchen.

"What are you eating?"

Everyone laughed at the sensitivity of their nostrils when food was involved.

Janita opened the door and shouted, "What's all the laughter about?"

Daddy Morgan said, "Come in and join us." Janita walked into the room, looked at Junior and Jeanette and said, "Ugh, you look like hell. Are you all just getting up?"

"No, we look like this all the time," Jeanette jokingly responded.

Julie, the peacemaker said, "Yes, they're just getting up. Now, Jeanette, move over to your place at the table."

Jeanette laughed, and said, "*MY* place. Oh, Lord, we're going back to our childhood. Girl, sit down in the other chair, or should I say sit down at my place."

157

Joseph quietly listened and observed his daughters in happy discussions but when he looked at his subdued son, their eyes met. Junior smiled and with so much admiration he whispered, "Thank you, Pop, for our family."

With those words, the laughter stopped and the room became extremely quiet.

Julie whispered, "I love all of you and I thank you for being there for me, not just recently but through all of my problems."

Jeanette said, "Okay, okay, enough of this mushy stuff, I need to hear some good gossip."

The family laughed and the conversations resumed.

Later, Janita questioned, "Pop, are you going to evening mass today?"

Julie replied, "I plan to go because I don't want to get up early tomorrow morning. Do any of you want to go with me?"

"Wouldn't it be nice to go to mass as a family today?"

All eyes turned to Jeanette and Junior to wait for their response. Feeling the stares from the family without looking up Jeanette said, "Don't forget to pray for us."

Janita said, "I know what I'm going to do. I'll pray and ask our poor dead mother who we know is in heaven to start working on your butts to get you back to church."

Jeanette said, "I go to church but not every Sunday and I pray daily. I don't have to be in God's house to pray."

Junior said, "I pray also, and I pray every day. And, you know what? My friend, my God hears me because he often answers my prayer."

Daddy Morgan said, "When you were young, your mother and I made sure you went to church, now as adults it's your decision how you take care of your soul. But, I'll tell you this; if I had a friend like you and if my friend never came to my house, sooner or later, I would stop visiting my friend."

Junior said, "Pop, I hear you."

Jeanette said, "But Pop, my friend, my God loves me and He knows that I love him."

Junior looked out doors and decided to change the discussion regarding church. "It certainly is a beautiful day and it may be a good time for a cookout, that is, if it's okay with Pop."

"Son, this is still your home so do what you'd like to do, but I don't plan to help you cook. However, I do plan to help you eat it."

Junior continued, "I promised Brandena that I would spend this afternoon with her and her sister, Katherine. I have a buddy that Brandena wants her sister to meet. I don't like playing match maker but the cookout may make it easier for me to introduce Stanley to Katherine."

"Junior, the cookout is a great idea and that will give me a reason to call Janita's classmate, Dexter, that I met last night."

"Oh, are you interested in Dexter?"

"Well, he seems very nice and he is different from most men that I've dated. For some reason he interests me."

"Girl, be careful of those poor men and I'm talking from experience."

Janita laughed and said, "Do you think you can live on a bartender's salary?"

Daddy Morgan said, "Baby, you couldn't live on a bartender's salary when you were in high school. You have always been able to throw money away."

Janita said, "Baby sister, don't worry about expenses because he has more than his salary."

Jeanette said, "Oh, really, what else does he have?"

The entire family looked at Janita to hear her response. "He has tips."

The family laughed. Jeanette said, "Cute, cute. Janita, I like him and I'm going to invite him over for Junior's cookout."

Junior said, "Jeanette, if you like that guy, call him. Don't worry about what Dexter says he does, the man does more than you think. Last night, when the TV was on the stock market channel, I observed him checking out the stock quotes. Later, I questioned him about several of the quotes that were being discussed on TV and the dude talked like a stock expert."

Daddy Morgan said, "Jeanette, if Junior is correct, that means your young man has money, so baby please leave him alone. You have the uncanny ability to send a rich man to the poor house."

The other three siblings laughed.

Julie said, "Pop, he may teach Jeanette how to manage money.

"Hallelujah! If that man can teach my baby girl how to save money, I'll personally invite him over for Junior's cookout."

The family laughed and all went their separate ways.

CHAPTER
THIRTY-ONE

"Dexter, this is Chief Petit. Son, I wanted to personally call you and thank you for helping the police department arrest the men who murdered Amber Lee. I know there're many unsung heroes in the world and you are certainly at the top of my list."

"Thank you, sir. I really appreciate your call. It means a lot to me."

"Son," the Chief continued, "if there is anything that we can do to help you, please let me know. Once again, thank you."

After the Chief hung up the phone, Dexter sat quietly for a few minutes and he felt really great but not because of the compliment but because the three worst enemies of Backatown were behind bars. Dexter's phone rang again and he thought, "Wow! I'm getting popular."

He picked up the telephone receiver and cheerfully said, "Yo."

"Yo," the sweet little voice on the phone repeated.

"Well, hello pretty lady. This is truly a surprise."

"Dexter, my brother is going to cook out this afternoon and I would like to invite you."

"Oh really. I would be happy to be your guest. What can I bring?"

"Yourself."

Dexter laughed.

"What do you drink?"

"White wine."

"I'll be there but I will need to know when and where?"

"We're still at Pop's place but some of the Morgans are going to Mass so I guess we should say about five thirty."

"Great," Dexter replied, "that'll also give me a chance to go to Mass. Jeanette, thank you for the invitation."

The smart mouth Jeanette said, "Let's wait and see if you'll thank me after you get to know me."

They both laughed and hung up the phone.

The shocked Jeanette could not believe what she just heard. She quickly pushed the mute button and screamed to Junior, "The man goes to Mass."

Junior laughed and said, "That's your Mom and your God answering your family's prayers."

CHAPTER
THIRTY-TWO

An aroma of breakfast cooking surrounded the entire Morgan house and Daddy Morgan was the guilty cook. Junior smelled the food and immediately arose to check it out.

"Good morning, Pop", Junior said, "the house smells like our old time Sunday mornings when you cooked breakfast for the family."

"Great, that's exactly what I had hoped for because it has been a long time since all of my children were home on a Sunday morning."

"Pop, when I first went away to school, the thing that I missed most in the family was our Sundays."

"I also missed the Sundays in the Morgan household," Jeanette added as she entered the kitchen. "By the way, Junior, your food was delicious last night."

"Thank you, Jeanette, but Pop wouldn't you agree that my food is always delicious?"

"Pop, don't go there because you might have to lie and today is Sunday."

As daddy Morgan laughed without commenting, Jeanette began to set the table as she did as a young girl. Watching his sister, Junior remembered that as a boy, it was his responsibility to pour the juice into the glasses and to place them in the correct spot on the table. Julie and Janita walked into the kitchen and after greeting the family the two sisters without any discussions began the tasks that their mother had assigned to them 20 years earlier. Janita toasted the bread, Julie set out the jelly and placed the serving dishes on the table after Daddy Morgan had placed the food into serving dishes.

Breakfast was ready and Joseph Morgan was thinking about Jacquelyn and missing his wife's presence more than he had in a long time. He moved to his chair at the table and to his surprise, Jeanette had set the sixth place on the table and had set a picture of her mother holding Amber on the place mat. Startled, Daddy Morgan smiled, sat down, and led the blessings. Looking at his children with tears in his eyes, he said, "Thank you. Thank you all. Now, let's eat!"

QUICK ORDER FORM

POSTAL ORDERS

Lepaugene' Enterprises
P.O. Box 640842
Kenner, La 70064

E-mail Address: Lepaugene @aol.com

PLEASE SEND THE FOLLOWING BOOK:
_____

MURDER UNDER THE WINDOW

Name:_____

Address:_____

City:_____

Telephone:_____

E-mail Address:_____

Cost of Book:_____$15.95_____

Shipping: US: $4 first book. $2 each additional book

     Intl: $9 first book. $5 each additional book